B.E

W9-BZW-240

3 9223 034985328

APR 2008

BLOOD
REDEMPTION

Other books by A. H. Holt:

Riding Fence
Blanco Sol
Kendrick
Silver Creek

BLOOD REDEMPTION

•

A. H. Holt

2

AVALON BOOKS
NEW YORK

Published by Thomas Bouregy & Co., Inc.
160 Madison Avenue, New York, NY 10016

Library of Congress Cataloging-in-Publication Data

Holt, A. H. (Anne Haw).
    Blood redemption / A. H. Holt.
        p.   cm.
    ISBN 978-0-8034-9890-7 (acid-free paper)
    I. Title.

PS3608.O494358B58   2008
813'.6--dc22   2007037210

PRINTED IN THE UNITED STATES OF AMERICA
ON ACID-FREE PAPER
BY HADDON CRAFTSMEN, BLOOMSBURG, PENNSYLVANIA

For my beautiful and brilliant sisters:
Jo Donovan and Edna Musser

Chapter One

Milt Anders jumped the four steps and hit the porch at a dead run. His boots heels rattled the oak boards. Grabbing the top of the swinging doors with both hands, he stuck his flushed face into the cool darkness of the Red Wheel Saloon and shouted, "Git out here, you sons! Red Thornton and Wes Lane are at it again. Hurry it up if you want to see anything. They're just past Pecan Hill and running flat out."

Boots pounded on the wooden floor of the saloon as five men jumped to their feet. The tall one knocked his chair over backward and spilled his beer as he joined the group running for the door. Pushing against one another to get through the swinging doors, they hurried out onto the porch to cluster around the still yelling Anders. Holding their hands flat over their eyebrows to shade their eyes, every man squinted into the late-afternoon sun.

Wes Lane's big palomino led Thornton's horse by at least a length. Long-legged and powerful, the horse stretched out, running his hardest. Anders laughed aloud and held his right arm out to point at the riders.

"Look at Wes Lane—slapping his horse's rump with that little whip he always carries."

Red Thornton's black appeared a lot smaller than the yellow horse. The sleek mustang stallion ran with his legs bunched close against his belly and his body low to the ground. A cloud of dust thrown up by the horse's hooves followed the racers.

As the riders approached the wooden bridge across Acorn Creek, the men could see Wes Lane's right arm swing high and slam down hard again and again. Every time the quirt struck the palomino's side, the horse flinched a little, almost breaking stride. Foam flecked the animal's pale nose and flew back against its shoulders.

The black ran steadily. His head was lower, but he gradually advanced until his nose looked almost even with the palomino's. The straining horses hit the bridge side by side. Their hooves slammed the thick oak planks, sounding like thunder. Red rode hunched forward, low over the black horse's withers, shouting encouragement and patting the animal's neck with his left hand.

When they hit the dusty street, the black ran nose to

nose with the larger horse. Still flailing wildly with his whip, Wes raked the straining palomino's sides with his big California spurs. Blood flew in a spattered arc across the horse's hindquarters.

The black lunged at least a full head out in front of the larger horse as they passed the group of men clustered on the saloon porch. After another hundred yards the racers passed the town well, and the smaller horse showed the palomino his rump.

Wes sawed on the reins and pulled his heaving horse to a stop. His face like a thundercloud ready to pour rain, he dismounted to stand stiffly in the middle of the street. He stared with angry eyes and his fists propped on his hips as Red slowed his black to a walk and turned to ride him back to the well, moving at an easy trot.

Stepping down from the saddle, Red led the black to the water trough, patting the animal's neck and shoulder and murmuring praises with every step. Trying to hide a grin, he kept his face turned away from Wes' angry stare.

"You cheated me again, blast your eyes, Red Thornton. That ugly piece of crow bait could never beat my palomino if you knew how to ride a fair race. You crowded me on the turn."

Red turned, lifting his head to look straight into the eyes of the tall, blond rider. "Face it, Wes, I didn't crowd you anywhere at all, and you know it. That oversized pony of yours is all show and no bottom. He starts off with a bang, but he's used up in half a mile."

"You just hold on 'til Coronado gets a blow, and I'll beat you on the way back—if that crow bait of yours don't crowd me."

Red laughed and shook his head as he said, "If you don't walk that horse some to cool him off, he'll not be fit to race again anytime soon."

Yanking the palomino's head up, Wes led the horse by the bridle reins as he walked toward the group of men still crowded around the saloon porch, discussing the merits of the race. He waved to a ragged boy hanging over the hitch rail.

"Here's two bits, boy. Walk my horse for me. Take him down to the bridge and back a couple of times. After he's cooled off good, give him about half a bucket of fresh water and tie him right here in front of the saloon."

Tossing his mount's reins to the boy, Wes stepped up onto the porch and stomped his feet as he swaggered through the crowd of men and pushed open the Red Wheel's swinging doors. Shaking his head and looking serious, he announced to anyone who would listen, "If Red Thornton ever ran a man a fair race, that black devil of a pony he rides wouldn't show a chance against my Coronado. You fellas shoulda seen how slick that boy did it. He guided his black close to Coronado so he could crowd me on that sharp turn down there by Lewis Gillium's place. I had to hold on as hard as I could to stay in the saddle. He almost put me and my horse both right over into the ditch."

Striding across the room to an empty table, Wes took

a seat facing the door and called to the bartender, "Give me two beers over here, Johnny. Red'll be in here in a minute—soon's he gets through babying that scrawny mustang of his."

Outside, Red let his horse drink a few mouthfuls of water, then pulled him away from the trough. "Take it easy, Pitch. You'll get plenty more water in a few minutes. You know better than to try to founder yourself—drinking too much when you're all hot from running. Come on now, you need to walk some more."

Leading the horse by a rein, Red walked up the street away from the Red Wheel. He turned left a few steps past the courthouse and headed toward the livery stable. Burt Glassner, the liveryman, came running from the direction of the saloon to catch up just as Red reached the open stable door.

Burt's face was red from exertion and he was chuckling as he said, "I saw the race, Red. I was in the Red Wheel getting me a cold drink with some of the fellas when old Milt Anders came running to the door. He yelled out that you and Wes was racing again, and everybody in the place got up and made tracks out to the porch so they could see the finish. This here black horse of yours sure can run."

"You're right there, Burt. This horse purely loves to run. Give him a bait of grain and a little more water, will you? Don't give him too much, now. He's just like any other fool of a horse and would drink too much if he could."

"I'll get old Nate to take good care of him for you, Red. Don't you worry about him none. I can't hardly get my hands on that horse without he gets all riled up, but he took to Nate the first time you ever left him here. He's as gentle as a lamb with him. You going over to the saloon now?"

"You bet I am—Wes owes me a beer, and I mean to collect."

Burt laughed and pushed his hat to the back of his bald head. "Wes Lane won't be none too happy that your horse beat his out. You can bet on that. He holds a lot of store by that big yellow horse of his'n. You're bound to the hurt his pride some beatin' him that way— right out in public like that. It's the second time you've done it too, ain't it?"

"Yeah, it's the second time I've done it. I know it hurts his pride to lose a race, Burt, but he asks for it. Heck, Wes plain out begs for it."

When Burt led Pitch through the wide end door of the livery stable, he held only the tips of the reins to stay as far from the horse as possible.

Nate hobbled over to grab the horse's bridle. "I seen the race too. This here cayuse can some kinda run."

"You got that right."

"Say, hold on there a minute, Red. I got a question for you."

"Sure thing, Nate. What is it?"

"I figure Burt's been living hereabouts more years

than God, so he could probably tell me, but I'd rather hear it from you. Why in the heck do folks call you Red? You ain't got red hair. Your hair's as black as that Indian's what runs around with your old man—that Chief Billy something."

"It's no big mystery, Nate. I was named after both of my granddads. One of them was William Lane, and the other was Rufus Thornton, so I'm really William Rufus Thornton," Red began.

"You coulda asked me that," Burt said. "I sure knew it. Both them names is downright famous around here. Them two fellas come in here together way back. They were tough old birds too. They cleaned out a nest of thieves and scoundrels that was using the valley for a hideout—followed them over the mountains on the old outlaw trail. After the crooks was gone, they took up land here, side by side.

"Red's granddad went by Bill, and his dad goes by Will, so they set out to call the boy Rufus—figured that would keep down the confusion. I guess the name didn't exactly fit, because it got turned into Red some kinda way, and it stuck."

"Well, I'll be swiggered," Nate said, a slight smile showing under his white mustache. "I figured you'd know, Burt. You know just about everything else."

Laughing softly, Red waved to the two men as he turned away to walk toward the saloon.

When he reached the porch, he placed one hand on

top of each of the swinging doors and pushed them open, stepping inside. The light in the room was poor, but the air felt several degrees cooler than outside.

As soon as he spotted Red standing at the door, Wes called out, "Come on over and sit down, partner. Here's the beer I owe you. I was beginning to think you were somewhere hiding your head in shame for winning a horse race the underhanded way you won it."

Winding his way through the tables, Red ignored the way the other patrons looked at him. Removing his hat, he dropped it onto a nearby table and settled in the chair directly across from Wes.

Careful to speak loudly enough for everyone to hear, Red said, "You keep on telling that tale over and over, Wes Lane, and you're gonna start to believe it your own self. I don't need to cheat none to beat you on a horse, and every man in Acorn Creek knows it—except you."

Wes raised both hands, palms out. "I know, I know, you're the best rider with the best horses in this part of Arizona Territory. I've heard it said more than enough times. I just don't believe it, that's all."

"Believe what you like. I know what I can do, and I know my stock. That saying you're quoting ain't so very wrong, either."

"Drink your beer, old son. I need to talk to you about those cattle you're moving for my old man."

Red lowered his voice. "Wes, Major Lane gave me my orders about what to do with those cattle. He even backed them up in writing. I've got his note right here in my pocket. I'm not thinking about doing a doggone thing with those cattle but exactly what your father wrote down here for me to do."

"You don't even know the deal yet, Red. You don't know anything about what I have in mind. You could at least listen to what I've got to say."

"That's true, Wes. I don't know the deal, and that's a fact. But you need to understand this before you start talking. I don't give a rat's hind end what you have in mind. I'm doing exactly what I agreed to do and not a thing besides.

"My orders are to roust a hundred steers out of that patch of woods near the creek bed behind your house, drive them to the railroad, and turn them over to Major Lane's factor, who'll be waiting down there to meet me. That's what your father said for me to do, and that's the end of it as far as I'm concerned."

"Come on, Red. Don't be like that. I need twenty of those cows—just twenty head. You can tell the major you tried but couldn't find the full hundred. He'll never know the difference."

"I'm not going to do that, Wes—you can just forget it. Stop talking about it. You're wasting your breath. I already told you this before we even left the ranch."

Wes leaned across the table and reached out to grab Red's right wrist in one long, slim hand. His face flushed with anger, and his voice grew louder. "You've got to help me, Red. You've just got to help me. Listen to me, man—just listen. Gil Patten will send some of those bully boys of his to hurt me. They'll do it too. Patten swore if I didn't place the money I owe him in his hands by noon this Sunday, he'd see I got two broken legs."

"Look, Wes, just stop it—stop talking about it. I can't do it. I just can't. Back off, for heaven's sake. I know I helped you the last time you got into trouble, but I can't do this. I won't do it. I don't have the money to lend you this time, and I won't do your father dirt. And that's the end of it."

Wes leaned forward to plead, "All you have to do is look the other way for a few minutes, Red—Bob Jenkins and me'll meet you down by the river crossing and cut twenty cows out of your herd. We'll drive them over to Cutter. I can sell them to that Mason Jones fella—the new man who's running the mine. Those miners are always needing beef."

Red shook his head and remained silent.

"Stop shaking your head at me, Red—please stop. You've got to listen this time. This is important. It may be life or death for me. You can't refuse me—you can't. You've got to help me."

Wes' face was covered in sweat, and his fingers tightened on Red's wrist. "Patten's men probably won't stop with breaking my legs. They'll likely try to kill me this time. You know they will."

Red yanked his wrist out of Wes' grip, pushed his chair back, and stood up, reaching for his hat. "I have to get home, Wes. You need to let this go—just forget it.

I'm not going to help you take twenty of Major Lane's cows. I don't care how much you talk or how sad your story gets."

Wes pushed his chair back and stood also. He rushed around the table to stand close to Red. His expression was grim. "Come on out back and talk to me about this, Red. There's another reason you've got to help me this time." Lowering his voice, he leaned closer to Red to whisper in his ear, "Becky's involved this time."

Red's face flushed, and his dark eyes seemed to flash with light when he heard Wes whisper Becky's name. He slammed his hat down onto his head with a jerky movement. His whisper sounded almost like a snarl. "Get out back right now, you everlasting weasel, and don't you say another word in here."

Red turned to stride through the back room of the saloon, out the door and down two stone steps to the gravelly dirt of the alley. Wes was right on his heels. Taking a few long steps away from the door so that no one inside the saloon could hear his voice, Red turned to face Wes, his hands on his hips.

"What the Sam Hill is the matter with you, Wes? You know better than that, for heaven's sake. How could you bring Becky's name up in there? Have you lost all your sense, all your decency?"

"Oh, calm yourself down, Red. Nobody but you heard what I said in there. The rest of those lazy bums weren't paying any attention to us."

"Like heck they weren't paying attention to us. Those two Dolman brothers sat right there at the next table, pop-eyed the whole time we were talking. They heard every blasted thing we said. They both plain jumped in their chairs when they heard you say Becky's name. I saw them do it."

"Well, I don't give a rip what those two clowns think about me or Becky McClain, either. So there."

"You'd better start caring, Wes, and start it fast. By golly, if you try that again, I'll teach you to care."

"Just shut up about it, Red. Talk to me about those cows. I've got to have the money to pay Patten, and you've got to help me."

"You might as well shut up about it yourself, Wes. I'm sorry, but it's like I've said over and over. I'm doing what I'm supposed to do and not one thing more."

Wes stepped closer to Red. His face gleamed white in the weak light, and his voice grew louder. "You'd let Patten's men work me over when all you have to do is look the other way long enough for me to drive a little jag of cows out of there? You know those cows partly belong to me."

"That's almost the same thing you told me back in June when you were so desperate for money, Wes. Remember? When you took most of my savings to get you out of the same sort of jam. Remember how you swore to me that if I would only help you, you'd never gamble again, and you'd return my money the next month? Well, I still don't have any money, and here you are in trouble for more gambling. I'm not falling for it again, Wes. You can just forget it."

Wes's face went from white to almost purple with anger. He suddenly lunged forward with his arms straight out and slammed both open hands against Red's chest, knocking him back against the building.

Caught completely unaware, Red lost his balance and fell sideways, sliding down the back wall of the saloon to strike his head on the sharp edge of the stone step. He rolled off the end of the steps and lay still, his body limp.

"Red?" Wes knelt beside the steps to stare into Red's still face, muttering to himself. "He's out like a light. Oh, but he's all right—he's still breathing."

Red groaned, his eyelashes fluttered, and he slowly moved one hand to the back of his head.

Wes rubbed his face with both hands, a desperate look in his eyes. "I thought sure he was dead," he whispered to himself.

Then he thought about that. "If Red was dead—if he got killed by some freak accident like this one, like falling down and hitting his head on that step—he couldn't stop me from getting some of those cows of Dad's and selling them to get the money I need to pay Patten."

Reaching past Red to feel around in the rubble beside the foundation of the building, Wes's fingers found a piece of granite almost as big as a water bucket. Using both hands, he raised the rock high over Red's face.

As his back and arms stiffened to smash the rock

straight down with all his strength, the back door of the saloon opened.

"What in the dickens are you fixing to do, Wes?" Johnny Yates yelled as the door slammed shut behind him. Yates started running down the steps. "What are you doing out here, you fool? Have you murdered that boy?"

Frightened and overcome by panic, Wes looked down. Red's pistol lay within an inch of his right hand. He yanked the gun out of Red's holster and turned to fire at the bartender.

The .44 bullet entered between Johnny Yates' eyes and took off most of the back of his head. He fell back against the saloon door and rolled off the far side of the steps.

Wes dropped the gun beside Red and ran for the saloon steps. He could hear the sound of boots striking the wooden floor as men rushed toward the door.

He yanked the back door of the saloon open with one hand and yelled at the top of his voice, "Somebody get Sheriff Logan and Doc Bailey over here fast! Red just killed Johnny!"

Red groaned again and put both hands on the ground to push himself to a sitting position. His head pounded. He forced his eyes open to see a crowd of men gathered around him. The alley suddenly seemed to be full of men. He could see Doc Bailey and Wes kneeling beside someone lying on the ground beyond the back steps of the saloon.

"What's happening?" Red muttered.

Sheriff Logan moved closer and squatted down in front of Red. "So you finally came to, huh? I thought you would—sooner or later. How many drinks did you have tonight, Thornton?"

Puzzled, Red lifted both hands to hold his aching head and whispered his answer, closing his eyes against the pain. "I had one beer—the same as usual, Sheriff. Why?"

"Ha. One beer. That's what they all say. You won't get away with this, though, doggone your sorry hide. Not a bit of it. You ain't gonna get crazy-mad drunk and shoot innocent people down like dogs in my town and get away with pretending you don't even know what you did."

"What in blazes are you talking about, Sheriff? You're the one who sounds drunk right now."

"Don't go getting yourself excited, Thornton. I've got your gun right here in my hand, and it's been fired. I can smell the burned powder plain as day. And Wes Lane stood within a few feet of you and watched you kill the man. You and him were the only ones out here, and he ain't even armed."

"Sheriff, this is crazy." Red struggled to get to his feet. "Anybody in town can tell you I never drink but one beer. Ask Johnny Yates—he'll tell you."

"It's poor old Johnny Yates you shot down, you miserable drunk. Straighten yourself up. I need to get you locked up for your own protection. People around here were fond of Johnny."

Motioning to Jack Dorman to move forward and take Red's left arm, Sheriff Logan pulled him forward.

Red lurched against the two men, still dizzy from his head's hitting the stone step. "Sheriff, wait. Listen to me. Please. I was knocked out. Wes and I were arguing, and he got excited and pushed me down. I didn't shoot anybody. I swear I didn't. I never even touched my gun. Get Doc Bailey to look at the back of my head—I'm still bleeding from where I hit my head."

"I see you've got some blood running down the back of your neck. You musta been so drunk, you fell over after you murdered poor old Johnny."

"You're not listening to me, Logan. I didn't shoot anybody. I haven't even touched my gun. Wes pushed me, and I fell and hit my head against those stone steps over there. The fall knocked me out for a few minutes."

"Stop your yammering, and move along, Thornton. You're still so drunk, you can't hardly stand up straight, much less talk sense." Giving a hard yank on Red's right arm, the sheriff dragged him through the crowd of men filling the alley.

Red's head cleared enough that he could see men he had always counted as friends and neighbors staring at him with hostile eyes. Still unsteady and confused, he held his head as high as he could and stared back.

As Jack Dorman and the sheriff pulled on his arms to lead him around the corner to Main Street, Red came face-to-face with Wes.

Wes stood in the middle of the street, surrounded by a group of cowboys from White Willow Ranch, waving his arms and talking.

Red called out to him, "Wes, come over to the sheriff's office and tell him how you pushed me and I hit my head on the step back there in the alley. He thinks I shot Johnny Yates."

Wes didn't answer. He stared at Red, his eyes as hostile as those of the other townsmen in the crowd. Still without answering, he watched as Jack Dorman and Sheriff Logan dragged Red away.

By the time they passed through the sheriff's office and reached the door with the iron-barred window to the jail's one cell, Red was feeling a bit steadier on his feet.

"Get in there," Dorman said, pushing Red toward the open door.

Catching himself against the low cot as he stumbled across the cell, Red turned to look at Dorman and said, "Jack, you know I wasn't drunk. You and your brother sat right there in the saloon no more than an arm's length from my table and listened to everything me and Wes said. You know as well as I do that I hadn't even finished drinking all of one beer when Wes and I went out back."

Without speaking, Dorman backed away from the cell door with his head down and refused to look at Red.

Sheriff Logan slammed the door so it latched and turned to grab Dorman's arm. "Hold it there a minute, Dorman. Is Thornton telling the truth about that beer? Were you sitting next to him and Wes the whole time? Is it true what he says? Did he only drink one beer?"

"I don't know, Sheriff Logan." Dorman pulled his arm out of the sheriff's grasp and raised his voice, a stubborn expression on his face. "I don't know nothing for sure. I didn't paid no never-mind to what Thornton did in there. All I could say for certain-sure is, he wasn't hardly in the Red Wheel long enough to get drunk, and I sure don't reckon he coulda been drunk while he raced that horse."

Shaking his head, Sheriff Logan turned away from Dorman to turn the key to lock the cell door. Raising his head, he peered through its barred window at Red. His voice sounded a little kinder.

"I'll ask questions, Thornton. Wes Lane's telling everybody you were so blind drunk, you pulled your gun and shot Johnny for no reason at all. He says he's the only witness to the shooting, and now you claim you were knocked out. Can you tell me any reason for Wes to shoot Johnny down like that and then turn around and blame it on you?"

Red sat down on the cot and held his throbbing head in his hands as he tried to think.

He finally lifted his head to look up at Logan and mutter, "I don't know, Sheriff. I just don't know."

Chapter Two

Red woke with the sun in his face.

What the devil? The sun doesn't come in through the window of my room. My room's on the west side of the house. Where in the Sam Hill am I? Where'd I spend the night?

Without moving, he looked around.

I remember now. I'm in the Acorn Creek jail. I'm in jail for murder—for shooting down an unarmed man. Shooting him down like a rabid dog.

That ain't all, either. Wes was there. Wes swore to Sheriff Logan and everybody who would listen that he stood there and watched me do the shooting.

When I passed him in the street, he looked at me like he hated me. He didn't even answer when I asked him to speak up for me.

Red sat up on the bunk, wincing at the crushing pain the movement caused. At first it seemed almost unbearable, sweeping down the back of his head and into his neck and shoulders.

Lord goodness, my head feels like somebody broadsided me with a shovel or something.

Sliding one hand around to the back of his head, Red felt a bump his long fingers could hardly cover. His hair was stiff, matted with dried blood at the nape of his neck. A thick bandage covered the entire back of his head.

I remember what happened now. Doc Bailey came over here last night and stitched my head up. He bandaged it like this. It's not so swollen—it's the bandages he put on it that stick out like that.

Leon Jackson, Sheriff Logan's deputy, opened the office door and stomped down the hall to look into the cell window, his expression unreadable. He held a tray covered in a white cloth against his shoulder with one hand.

"Here's your breakfast, Thornton. It should still be hot. That cute little sister of Becky McClain's fetched it over here for you. You must really rate high with that girl. She said there wouldn't be no charge for it.

"I didn't bother nothing, but I took the cloth off and looked it over good. It's my job to look things over like that. I got to make sure she didn't try to sneak you in a gun or some other kind of weapon.

"Women are all the time up to some fool trick like

that, trying to get their men out of jail. I'll set it down here on the floor while I open the door."

"Thanks, Leon. Next time you see Jeannie, please tell her I said thanks. Tell her I said it was mighty kind of her to think of me."

"You think that kid's got her eye on you, Red?" Leon grinned as he reached through the open door to hand Red the tray.

"Oh, for heaven's sake, Leon, Jeannie McClain ain't much more than a baby. She's just being nice, is all."

"She ain't all that much of a baby no more, if you ask me." Leon hesitated, then grinned as he said, "I noticed Miss Becky didn't come over here with no breakfast for you. I thought *she* was your girl."

"You know good and well that's none of your business, Leon. I'd take it as a favor if you'd leave it alone."

"I didn't mean nothing, Red. Only I did see Miss Becky ride out of town with Wes Lane right after daybreak this morning."

Red looked down at the tray of food and turned his back on Leon. The deputy stood in the doorway a second or two as if he wanted to say more. He finally sighed and stepped out of the cell to slam the door.

Red couldn't help but shudder when he heard the key click in the lock.

Sitting on the cot with the tray in his lap, he ate two biscuits with gravy and three fried eggs, gulping down the lukewarm coffee between bites.

I was about starved. I musta missed my supper last

night. This food is sure a blessing. My head's sore as the devil, but it's surely gonna stop pounding pretty quick. I can at least think clearly again—part of the time, anyway.

I think I remember feeling Wes' hands tugging at my gun belt. It was right after that when I heard the shot. It musta been the shot that killed Johnny.

If nobody else was in the alley with us, it had to be Wes who shot Johnny. I wasn't in any kind of shape to pull a gun or shoot anybody about that time. But my gun was out of my holster, and it was fired, so if it wasn't me who done it, it had to be Wes. There's no other explanation.

My head hurt me so much about then, I got completely befuddled. But I know I'd never get confused enough to shoot Johnny Yates. Heck-fire, it's troublesome enough for me to shoot coyotes or a calf with a broken leg.

I'd probably have a hard time shooting at somebody threatening me. I know good and well I didn't fire my gun last night. I know I didn't shoot Johnny.

That only leaves Wes. It had to be Wes.

He's not here to side with me, so he musta done it, and now he's blamed it on me. Only, why in the world would he do such a thing? It's just plain hard to believe.

He must be scared to death of that Gilbert Patten and his bunch to do such a thing and then up and blame it on me. We ain't been so very close lately, but I'm his first cousin—his only cousin, far as I know.

Maybe I'm just still confused. Maybe I shouldn'ta eaten those eggs. My stomach don't feel so good.

After sipping the last of the cooling coffee, Red muttered to himself, "I reckon Wes'll get his way about those cows now."

Sleepy, he set the tray on the floor and lay down on the cot.

"Wake up, Thornton!" Sheriff Logan yelled. He looked through the little window in the door to the cell. "You've been sleeping for three days."

Red struggled to a sitting position. "That's a crock. I have not been sleeping for three days. I've been asking to get to talk to you every day, but that thickheaded Leon Jackson always says you're too busy to bother with me."

"I am busy. I'm the sheriff in this town, remember? Doc Bailey's here to see you again."

"How're you doing, Doc? My head's okay now."

"I'll be deciding that for you, son. I've got to check those stitches I put into your scalp anyway."

The doctor turned to look up at the sheriff. "Hurry up and open the door, Logan. I don't have all day for this."

"Hey, take it easy there, Doc. The door's open."

As Bailey stepped into the cell, Logan slammed the door and relocked it. He rattled a big bunch of keys to emphasize his words. "Yell when you're finished here, and I'll come let you out."

Ignoring Logan, Doc Bailey dropped his bag onto the cot. "Lean forward a little, Thornton. This might hurt some, but I'll go easy. I've got to pull this bandage off to check the stitches and put on a clean one.

"That was a nasty blow you took, and you've had a serious concussion. I explained to Sheriff Logan that you were obviously out of your head when you shot Yates. I told him I'd testify to that at your trial.

"It's plain to me by the way you've been sleeping so much and having those spells of nausea, you sustained a dangerous blow to your head. Something like that can completely confuse a man."

Red leaned away and turned his head to look up into Bailey's face. "I didn't shoot Johnny Yates, Doc. I was knocked out for a few minutes there that night, but I know I didn't shoot my gun."

"It's all right, son." Bailey patted his shoulder and looked sad. "Sheriff Logan and the town prosecutor are only charging you with manslaughter. Judge Sellers won't give you more than five years in prison, if he gives you that much."

"You're not listening, Doc." Red raised his voice a little and stood up to look down at Bailey. "I said I did not shoot the man. Wes lied to everybody. I can't think why he would, but he used my gun to shoot Johnny while I was still knocked for a loop from hitting my head on that stone step."

"I can see you believe truly that, Thornton, but nobody else in town is going to. You might as well face it."

"My head's still spinning, Doc. I'll tell you what—I can't hardly believe this is happening."

"Well, buck up, son. It's bad, I know, but you're young and strong. You'll outlive this."

Without saying anything more, Doc Bailey finished checking the stitches in Red's head and applied a smaller bandage. Putting his equipment back into his black leather bag, he pounded on the wall and called for Sheriff Logan to open the door.

Leon appeared almost immediately with the key.

Red almost shouted. "Where's Sheriff Logan now?"

"Keep your shirt on, Thornton. The sheriff's busy, like I done told you over and over. You ain't going nowheres anyway, so don't get yourself in a snit about it. He'll get to you when he gets doggone good and ready to get to you."

"You go soak your head, Leon. Tell Sheriff Logan I want to talk to him."

"You've got more visitors, Thornton. Your pa and that there Indian of his'n are waiting out front."

"Well, are you going to let them come in anytime soon?"

"I'm thinking on it. You've got no call to get so fierce with me, Thornton. I'm gonna let them in to talk to you, but I thought if I waited a little spell before I let 'em in, you might learn to keep a civil tongue in your head."

"You get out of here, you little sawed-off imitation of a grown-up man. I'll get my hands on you one of these days." Red moved to the bars on the window and looked out at Leon. "You just go out there and let my dad and his friend Billy in, Leon Jackson. Sheriff Logan is going to get back here and talk to me someday.

I'm not a bit too proud to tell him about your little meannesses."

"He'll never believe anything you say about me, Thornton. You're nothing but a drunk and a murderer."

Red didn't answer. Holding the bars of the window with both hands, he stared into Leon's face until the deputy lowered his eyes and turned away.

Almost as soon as Leon closed the office door, he opened it again and held it back against the wall for Will Thornton and Chief Billy Two Horses to enter the hallway in front of Red's cell.

Reaching out through the bars, Red clasped his father's fingers with his right hand and held his left out to Chief Billy.

Tears glimmered on Will Thornton's cheeks. "We got here as soon as we could, son. The oldest Dolman boy came out to the house and told us you were locked up in here for getting drunk and shooting poor old Johnny Yates.

"I told the boy to his face he was telling me a dad-blasted, malicious lie. I told him you couldn't be forced to drink enough to get yourself drunk—not even if somebody used a bullwhip on you—and he ought to know it.

"Dolman hemmed and hawed some, but he finally promised me he'd come in and testify at your trial. He admitted he sat at a table next to you in the Red Wheel that night. He promised me he'd swear you didn't even finish drinking all of one glass of beer."

"Thanks, Dad. Maybe that'll help some. The sheriff and everybody else in town is convinced I got myself so drunk, I shot Johnny down without even knowing what I was doing."

"That no-account Wes Lane is going around town telling the story exactly like that, son. He tells everybody he can get to listen to him that he woulda stopped you if he coulda grabbed your gun, but you moved too fast for him.

"I told you time after time not to fool with that boy, son. He's damaged in some kind of way—always has been. I reckon he coulda been born thataway, but his thinking just ain't exactly right. It never has been."

"You can say that again," Billy interrupted, raising his voice. "I told you before too, Red. Wes got born with no conscience—no conscience at all. On top of that, he's a low-down, sneaking coward, and everybody knows, a coward is the most dangerous kind of man in all Creation."

"I know, Billy, I know. You've been telling me all that for as long as I can remember, and you've darn sure been proven right by this. I just always believed I could help Wes—that he would eventually straighten out if we showed him enough patience. But this—this is plain unbelievable."

Red paused and shook his head. "I've been sleeping off this knock on my head and gradually remembering everything that really happened the other night. Wes and I were arguing something fierce when we went out back of the saloon. He kept on begging me to let him cut out twenty head of the major's cows to sell over to the mine."

"Go on," Will prompted him.

"He needed money to pay Gilbert Patten some more gambling debts he'd run up. I told him no. I told him no over and over. He kept on whining and begging until I got up from the table to leave. He jumped up then and came over to whisper in my ear that Becky McClain was involved some kind of way."

Again Red shook his head. "When he mentioned Becky's name, I made him come out into the alley to talk. When we got out there, he kept right on begging. When I still wouldn't agree to help him, he finally got so agitated, he slammed me in the chest with both hands.

"He hit me so hard, he knocked me back against the wall of the saloon. It was then that I lost my balance and fell sideways against the stone steps going up to that little back stoop. The fall knocked me out for a few minutes."

"Are you all right now, son?"

"I'm fine, Dad. I promise, I am. Doc Bailey said my head must be harder than a rock. He put about fifteen stitches into it for me. I'm only a little sore now. He came around a little while ago and checked the stitches. He says it's healing fine. But let me finish my story."

Will Thornton nodded his assent, and Red continued. "I felt groggy when I woke up. I wasn't out but a minute or two. I opened my eyes to see Wes holding a rock as big as a watermelon. He had it up in both hands, right over top my face. My guess is he planned to use it to bash my head in. It doesn't make much sense, but that's all I can think.

"About the time I looked up and saw that rock, Johnny Yates came out the back door of the saloon and yelled at Wes.

"Johnny's yell surprised Wes, and I reckon it shook him so much to know that Johnny saw him holding the rock over my head, he turned and threw the rock aside.

"Almost in the same motion, he grabbed my gun out of my holster. He raised it and shot the poor man without even saying another word.

"It didn't seem to me like he even took time to think. He dropped the gun onto the ground beside me and started running. He dashed in the back door of the saloon, screaming for somebody to get the sheriff. He told everybody in earshot how I killed Johnny Yates."

Billy Two Horses almost hissed as he said, "I'll kill the stinking little sidewinder with my bare hands."

"Calm yourself down, Billy. I need you to help Dad. If you go after Wes, something could go wrong, and then Dad would be left alone. They've got me sewn up right and tight. I'm not gonna get out of here anytime soon.

"That means I'm not going to be able to get the money we need to pay the drovers to take care of the stock this winter. I had that job of moving cows for Major Lane lined up. It woulda paid me enough to see us through, but it's a bust now."

"Don't you be thinking anything about such stuff, boy. We've got plenty of time after you get out of this cage." Will Thornton's voice was shaky.

"Dad, please. We've got to face facts. Sheriff Logan, Doc Bailey, and the rest of the town believe I shot Johnny Yates in a drunken stupor. Wes is going around swearing he stood there and watched me do it.

"Even my memory about what really happened in the alley is a little hazy. All I can really say is, I know I didn't shoot the man. But I don't have any proof of anything.

"If I say I remember seeing Wes shoot the man, it only looks like I'm really guilty and trying to throw blame off onto him.

"Johnny was shot with a .44. I was the only person in the alley carrying a .44. When the sheriff got there, it was plain my gun had been fired in the last few minutes." He shrugged helplessly. "To be honest, I think I'll be lucky not to get hanged."

"My Lord, son. What can you do? What can I do?"

"There's not much I can see to do, Dad. Doc Bailey says he'll testify I didn't know what I was doing because of a concussion. He told me today I'll only be charged with manslaughter. If that's true, at least I don't have to worry about getting hanged for something I didn't do."

"I'll get you a lawyer and stay here in town with you, Red. Maybe we can find a way to prove you didn't do this."

"Dad, I think you and Billy should go on back home. You need to get the hands to drive the cattle back into the hills, then pay 'em their time. That's the only way you'll be able to buy enough supplies for you and Billy to make it through this winter. You two can care for the horses without any help."

"I'm not leaving you until I know what's going to happen. Soon's I leave here, I'll go talk to Ben Seymour. He'll do all he can for you."

"I don't want you to spend what little money we've got paying a lawyer to try a lost cause. I can face whatever they deal out to me, Dad. Keep the money to buy supplies and grain for those mares. Their foals are our future."

"Don't you go worrying none about your pet horses, Red," Billy said. "Me and Thorn here can care for your stock same as you can, boy. I'll run them up to my place on Heard's Mountain. I can go on up there now and get the place shipshape, and soon's this trial is over, we can all take the horses and move up there."

Suddenly alert, Red looked from Billy to his father. "What's going on? Why do you want to do that? What's happened to make you suggest moving away from the ranch?"

Will gave Billy a hard look and said, "There's been some fence cutting, and somebody run off a little jag of cows a couple of days ago. The dogs chased two or three fellas away from the back corral last night. We left both of the Sloan boys patrolling the place with their rifles and let the dogs run loose when we left to come see you."

"Do you have any idea who it was?"

Billy almost yelled, "My best guess is it was Wes Lane and some of that Patten crowd."

"Aw, come on, Billy. Wes?"

Billy jumped up from his squatting position and began to pace the hall, his long braids swinging. "You always were a fool about that cousin of yours. He's just put a noose around your neck, and you don't want to believe he'd steal your blasted horses if he could? What's the matter with you, boy?"

"I guess you're right, Billy. Of course you're right. I guess it's just an old habit for me to look after Wes.

"I know Wes can't be trusted—I do see that plain enough—but why would he try to steal my horses? Everybody around here knows they're mine. He couldn't use 'em or even sell 'em to anybody unless he took 'em somewhere clean out of the Territory."

"Of course he could sell the horses, boy. Don't act more of a fool than you have to. He'd make up some tale about your giving 'em to him or his taking them to pay a debt you owed him or something. If not that, he'd take them far enough away from here so he could sell 'em where nobody knows where they came from."

"Maybe you're right about the horses. I just don't know. I do know this much Billy—Dad's got no business staying up on Heard's Mountain over a winter with his rheumatism as bad as it is. He'll be crippled up in a week of really cold weather in that cabin of yours."

"That just goes to show how little you know, boy. I can keep my cabin warmer than you ever kept that big old board house of yours. I'll see that Thorn stays warm."

"Don't you two keep talking like I ain't even here." Will reached over to shove Billy with his left hand. "Red, Billy's gonna go ahead back home and tend to things there. I'll stay in town until your trial is over."

"Dad, do me a favor. I know you don't like Becky McClain, but I'm worried about her. Please try to find out if she's all right."

"You mean to tell me she ain't been here to see you yet, and her living right here in town? The sorry girl does that, and you still want to go chasing after her?"

Red stepped back and waved both hands in front of him. "Forget what I said, then—just forget about it. I'll send word to her sister. She'll tell me about Becky. Just forget I said anything."

"I'm sorry, son. I'm sorry. But I hear things. That girl is bad medicine. She's way too thick with Wes Lane and that Gilbert Patten gang."

"Wes hinted to me last night that Becky was in some kind of danger from Gilbert Patten and his men."

"I'm sure she is, but not the kind of danger the low-down weasel wanted you to think. I'll ask around about her, son. I'll let you know what I find out." Will paused. "You're right in thinking I don't like the girl. I don't like her one bit, and that's a fact, but I know you do, so I'll find out what I can."

"Thanks, Dad. I appreciate it."

"Come on, Thorn," Chief Billy said, starting back down the hall. "Let's get out of this place. It's giving me the heebie-jeebies. I'd like to get those supplies bought and make tracks back to the ranch before it gets dark."

"Go to the livery and get Pitch, Billy—please. Tell Burt I sent you after him. Take him with you to the high country. If Wes or Patten or anybody else wanted one of my horses, it would surely be that stud horse."

"I'll get me a new rope so I can make me a long lead. That devil of a horse don't like me one bit," Chief Billy grumbled.

"Don't feel bad about it, Billy. It's surely nothing personal. I think Pitch hates almost everybody in the whole world outside of me and maybe old Nate at the livery. For sure can't anybody else ride him—he carries on like a wild mustang every time anybody tries."

"He's more'n half wild mustang at that. Don't you worry none about your pet horse. I'll get him back with those mares, and he'll be happy as a cow in clover."

Red felt a pang of loneliness when the door to the office slammed shut behind his father and Chief Billy. He stood still for several minutes, holding the bars in the small opening with both hands.

After a while he walked over to flop down onto the narrow cot and shut his eyes, hoping he could go back to sleep so his head would stop hurting.

Will Thornton and Chief Billy Two Horses stood on the boardwalk in front of the jail without speaking for several minutes. Both men stuffed their hands into their pockets and held their heads down, stunned.

"You go on out to the ranch, Billy," Will said finally. "I'm going to have a talk with Doc Bailey. It's plain enough to see Red's not right—not right at all. He acts like he's in some sort of a trance and slurs his words when he talks. I figure that blow to the head hurt him a lot more than he thinks."

"That has to be it, Thorn. That boy ain't proper upset for a body sitting in jail waiting on a hanging or to be sent off to Yuma. Seems like to me he should be all fired up—at least plenty fired up at that low-down, sorry Wes Lane.

"I'm gonna see if I can't find that skunk before I leave town. He'll not get away with doing that boy like this."

"Well, I don't think Wes is in town right now. Anyway, it would be better if you would go on out to the ranch, Billy, and get the cattle moving. I'll try to see Doc Bailey and get that lawyer started on doing what he can for Red."

Chapter Three

The days ran together like water poured into a pond.

Red slept for hours every day. He'd been locked in the jail cell for eleven days when Judge Sellers rode into town. Still dressed in his traveling clothes, the judge came into the jail and looked at Red without speaking, then left. He announced around town that Red's trial would be held at ten o'clock on Monday morning, two days later.

Sheriff Logan brought Red a clean shirt, a basin of hot water, and shaving gear. He opened the cell door to bring them in, handed the shirt to Red, and set the basin on the floor and the shaving gear up on the window ledge.

"Git over here and clean yourself up, son. The jury'll

think you're an outlaw for sure if they see you sporting such a growth of beard and wearing a dirty shirt with bloodstains running down the back."

"I'm obliged to you, Sheriff. It'll feel good to get cleaned up. I don't know how much it'll help with the jury, though." Red looked at the shirt. "Who brought me this new blue shirt? It sure isn't one of mine."

"Major Lane bought it over to the mercantile. He was good enough to ask me what all you needed for the trial. I think it was mighty fine of him, considering."

"Considering his own son is gonna lie to get me hanged?"

"Wes Lane's story is the only evidence we've got, Thornton, and you haven't told me anything to prove what he says is a lie. The jury's sure to find you guilty." He hesitated. "But even if the jury does find you guilty, you're only charged with manslaughter. That's not a hanging offense. I'm thinking you'll most likely get five to ten years in Yuma prison."

Red sighed and shook his head, turning away from Sheriff Logan to stare out the cell's one narrow window.

"Don't go getting yourself down now, Thornton. You're young, and you'll survive this. I know it's hard, but it was some harder for poor old Johnny Yates."

"Sheriff, I'm telling you again. I did not shoot Johnny Yates."

Logan turned his face away and almost shouted, "Get

yourself clean and shave, so I can take that razor out of here. I ain't got all day to stand here yammering with you. It ain't but about twenty minutes before you've got to be in that courtroom."

With the sheriff holding his left arm, Red led the way through the alley to the back steps of the courthouse. They entered the rear door and walked along the hall to the courtroom. People stood in ragged groups along the length of the hallway, talking. When they heard the door close and saw the two men step inside, the talking stopped, and everyone turned to stare.

When Sheriff Logan opened the door to the courtroom, Red could see that every seat was filled. People stood two deep against the wall at the back of the room. He couldn't help but think of vultures gathering around the carcass of a dead calf.

The whole trial took less than two hours.

Sheriff Logan took the stand first. He testified to finding Johnny Yates lying dead near the back door of the saloon with half his head blown away by a .44 slug.

He swore he found the gun lying on the ground near Red's left hand, and it was recently fired, because it smelled of burned powder.

Wes Lane held his right hand on the Bible and swore to tell the truth. He settled into the witness chair and testified that he had watched with horror as, in a drunken stupor, Red Thornton pulled his handgun and deliberately shot down Johnny Yates for no reason at all.

Doc Bailey sat up on the stand and swore Red was so drunk that night and so severely concussed from the blow to his head, he didn't even know what he was doing when he shot Johnny.

Jack Dolman was true to his word. He came forward to get on the stand and swear with his hand on the Bible that Red wasn't in the Red Wheel Saloon long enough to get drunk that day. He said that, as far as he knew, Red only drank part of one glass of beer.

Attorney Benjamin Seymour stepped forward to tell the jury Red's story. "My client is innocent of this charge. He did not fire his gun. He did not remove it from his holster. Before Johnny Yates came into the alley, Red Thornton and Wes Lane were arguing. Lane lost his temper and pushed Red, so he fell against the stone steps at the back of the saloon, striking his head. The blow knocked him unconscious."

He paused for emphasis. "When Red came to, his gun lay in the dirt beside him, and Sheriff Logan stood over him. He was not drunk, and he did not fire his pistol. Someone else fired it and killed Johnny Yates."

There were no more witnesses, and the jury filed out.

In less than thirty minutes the twelve men came back into the courtroom, and the foreman announced their verdict, finding Red guilty of manslaughter. Judge Sellers slammed his gavel down on his desk as he sentenced

William Rufus Thornton to serve three to five years at hard labor in Yuma prison.

Sitting beside Seymour at the big oak table, Red slumped down in his chair, his head aching. When the jury foreman read the verdict, Red stared at Wes, hoping his cousin could feel his eyes on him.

Wes didn't look Red's way, not once. He kept his eyes carefully averted, never glancing Red's way, not even when he sat in the witness chair and lied to condemn his cousin as a murderer.

Red felt his father's hand on his shoulder.

Turning to speak close to Will's ear so he could be heard over the hubbub, Red spoke quickly. "I'll be all right, Dad. I promise. I want you to go on home now and help Billy. The sheriff will be taking me to Gila Bend on the stage. I'll wait there for a few days before I go on to Yuma."

He could hear tears in his father's voice. "They'll kill you in that awful place, son. They'll drag you down there in that iron prison wagon and kill you."

"They won't kill me, Dad. I'll be all right. I promise you. I'll put up with whatever I need to and get back here as fast as I can. You and Billy keep yourselves safe and watch out for my horses. Don't be sitting around worrying about me every minute. I'll make it through this. I'll work hard and be careful. You just go on and take care of yourself."

"I can't hardly believe this is happening to us, son."

"It's hard, I know. But it's surefire real, and that's a fact. Go on now, Dad, please. Sheriff Logan wants to take me back over to the jail. He keeps on looking at us, and I know that's what he wants."

"You write to me—you promise you'll write to me," Will insisted.

"I've already promised you about fifty times I'd write. I'll write you as often as I possibly can. Sheriff Logan will give you directions for sending a letter to the prison, and you be sure to send me a blank sheet of paper every time you write. I'll send you my answer right off. You can pay the postage when the letters arrive. I don't reckon I'll be allowed to have any money for mailing letters out of the prison."

Sheriff Logan pushed his way through the crowd and reached out to grasp Red's elbow as he stood up. "Come on, boy. We'd better go around the back way again to the jail. There's a lot of ugly talk going on out in front of the courthouse. Some of the men around town think you got off a mite too easy."

"Did you bother to tell them I'm innocent?"

"Oh, for heaven's sake, Thornton, will you shut up about that? The jury found you guilty. That's the only truth I've got to deal with."

Red didn't say any more and stayed close to Sheriff Logan as they walked through the narrow hallway behind the courtroom and out the back door of the courthouse.

Logan continued to hold Red's arm with one hand as

he led him through his office and back to his cell. Pushing Red through the opening, he slammed the door and locked it.

Almost numb with the shock at the swiftness and finality of the trial and sentencing, Red dropped down onto the bunk and leaned back against the wall.

It's hard to even think I keep telling Dad everything's all right, but I'm scared half to death. I think I must still be a little thick from that blow my head took against those steps. It feels like I should wake up—I should wake up, and, when I do, all this'd be no more than a muddled-up dream.

Two days after the trial, Billy Two Horses came to the jail with a bundle of clean clothes and Red's winter jacket. Sheriff Logan checked the bundle for weapons and told Billy he'd keep the clothes in his office and give them to Red so he could wear them the day he left on the stage.

The stage pulled out of Acorn Creek early. Jeannie McClain brought Red his breakfast, the same as she'd brought it every day he was locked in the jail. She never came in to see him but always left the tray with Leon. That morning she left him a basketful of food and a jug of coffee to take on the stage.

Becky McClain never came to see him.

Cleanly shaved and dressed in fresh clothes, Red stepped out into the gray morning. Nobody except the stage driver was on the street. Sheriff Logan held Red's arm with one hand as they exited the front door of his office, walked across the dirt street, and stepped up into the stage.

As they were leaving the jail, Sheriff Logan whispered to Red, "I'll leave the handcuffs and leg irons off for now, Thornton, if you'll give me your word you won't try to escape."

"You have my word, Sheriff. All I want is to get this nightmare over and done with. I'm still so wobble-headed, I wouldn't be able to run anywhere if I tried to get away, anyway."

There were no other passengers. They'd have at least the first part of the journey to themselves. Red lay his head back on the seat and let his thoughts drift.

It ain't that I haven't entertained the idea of trying to escape. I've thought of it about every hour on the hour—every hour I've been awake, anyway. I know I wouldn't take the chance, though, not even if it was handed to me.

I've got Dad and Billy to think about, the start of a horse herd waiting for me to come back to. And there's Becky McClain. Becky said once we might get married someday, if I'm not just dreaming. Maybe I shouldn't think about Becky too much, but she's a lot to come back for.

It's plain enough, though—yeah, it's plain to me that if I was fool enough to try to escape, even if I made it and got clear, I'd be throwing everything away—everything.

The rocking motion of the stage made Red's head

hurt. After a few miles his nausea came back. The same nausea he'd suffered the first days after his fall in the alley. The feeling had cleared up some in the last few days, and he'd hoped it was gone for good.

Holding his head with both hands, he closed his eyes and leaned back against the upholstered seat. *Will this upset feeling never end? I'm still cloudy-headed, and now I'm ready to start puking again.*

When he opened his eyes, Sheriff Logan stared at him from the opposite seat. "I'm glad we could travel alone like this, Thornton. It's easy enough to see your head's still hurting you."

Red said nothing.

"Old Jacob Pritchard will have you in wrist and leg irons soon's I turn you over to him down at Gila Bend. He keeps a prisoner thataway 'til he hands him over to the guards at Yuma."

The sheriff paused, then said, "Doc Bailey says you ain't in no fit shape to try anything reckless yet, anyways."

"I'm obliged, Sheriff. You can stop worrying about me trying anything. I gave you my word I wouldn't try to escape, and I won't. I feel so low now, I couldn't do it if I wanted to."

"Come on and wake yourself up then. You look some better since you shaved again and put on clean clothes, but you're still about as pale as my grandma's fresh-bleached bed linen. It appears to me you've slept most of the time we've been riding."

"My head's been hurting right bad, Sheriff, but it's better now. I reckon I'll live—long enough to get to Yuma at least."

"You'll be all right there, boy. You just make up your mind to take what comes and live through it."

Logan stared into space for a moment. "My own daddy was flung down into a cave prison, way up north there in Connecticut or some such place after he was captured in the War. He stayed in that infernal hole a full two years without even a peep at the sky, and they worked him like a slave. He walked around with irons on his ankles the whole time."

The Sheriff shook his head before continuing. "Daddy said some fellas that were put in that prison at the same time he was went plumb crazy after a while. But he figured he had it to do, so he buckled down and made it through, hour by hour."

Logan shook his head again and smiled wistfully. "He come home to us too. He looked thin as a rake and was bad sick when he got there, but he made it. Ma took care of him and fed him up until he got well again. You can do it too. You'll at least get plenty of food, and you'll work outside in the sunshine down at Yuma."

Listening to the sheriff talk, Red slipped off to sleep again.

The sun streamed in through the coach window when Red woke again. Clearly, hours had passed since they left Acorn Creek. Stretching his arms and legs and rubbing his stiff neck, he looked at Sheriff Logan and muttered, "I wish I could stop this everlasting sleeping all the time."

Pushing his hat back to uncover his eyes, Logan straightened up in his seat opposite Red and said, "Doc Bailey said you were sleeping all the time because of that whack you got on the back of your head. It did something to your brain."

"Well, I sure need you to get this coach to stop pretty quick, or I'm liable to throw up all over you."

"Well, for heaven's sake, just hold your water."

Logan pounded on the roof of the coach with one fist. The stage lurched and swayed from side to side as the horses broke stride and the driver pulled them to a stop. Logan slammed the door back against the side of the coach and climbed out to turn around and hold one hand up to help Red to the ground.

"Grab that basket, Thornton. If you eat whatever food Jeannie McClain packed for you, you might get to feeling better."

"I don't know about eating anything, Sheriff. The thought of food makes me feel even worse than I felt before. Maybe it'll help if I just sit on something that holds still for a few minutes."

"When we get going again, you sit over in the seat facing forward. I've heard people say that riding with your back to where you're going makes some folks get stomach sick even when they're well, and it's plain your head ain't got over that blow yet."

"You eat the lunch, Sheriff, and take the empty basket back to Jeannie. You could tell her how much I appreciated it, if you would."

"I'll just do that. You lean back against that tree and get you some rest. Me and the stagedriver need us a break, same as you."

Chapter Four

Red slept the rest of the trip and only woke up when Logan grasped his left shoulder and shook him as they entered the town.

Pritchard didn't look up when Sheriff Logan handed Red over. He held a hand out to take the papers Logan handed him. Barely looking at them, he stuffed them into a pocket and turned to wrap a hard hand around Red's arm as he drew his Colt and cocked it with his other hand.

Only then did he turn to speak to Logan. "I done told you about bringing me prisoners without irons, Logan. It ain't right. One of these days one of your pet hard cases is gonna kill somebody trying to escape. I don't figure on it being me."

Turning away from Logan's attempt to explain that

Red was too ill to try to escape, Pritchard shoved the barrel of the pistol into Red's back and growled, "Don't you go trying anything, boy. Just move along. You can see the blacksmith right ahead of you yonder. I figured Logan might not have you ironed, so the smith's over there waiting on you with his forge nice and hot."

Gritting his teeth, Red lowered his head and closed his eyes to shut out the sight of the iron bands the smith fitted around his wrists and ankles. The sound of every blow of the man's hammer seemed to cut through his head.

Once the irons were secure, the smith fitted a light chain between Red's ankles and another between his wrists. The weight of the iron bands and the chains dragged down his arms and made it difficult to walk. He could only take short, dragging steps.

"Get movin', convict." Pritchard's harsh voice raked Red's ears. "Climb up in here. I ain't got forever to get going." He chuckled harshly. "You're lucky, boy. There ain't but one other prisoner on this trip, and he don't look to be the kind to bother you. You'll probably make it all the way to down to Yuma without getting beat up or worse."

The prison wagon was no more than an iron cage on axles. It was the size of an ordinary farm wagon but had oversized wheels. The bed of the wagon contained what appeared to be clean wheat straw. The cage looked big enough to carry eight or ten men lying down. The only other prisoner sat in a corner near the front of the cage. His head drooped to his chest, and he didn't seem to notice Red.

Red climbed into the cage and, stooping over, worked his way to the rear to sit in a corner facing the horses. He leaned his head back against the iron bars. The other prisoner didn't move. The straw did little to soften the rough jostling of the wagon. Still, Red was asleep before the wagon left town.

I can hear people talking, and something smells funny. I wish they would be quiet. If I open my eyes, my head will start hurting again. My eyelids feel glued together, anyway.

The light's too bright—somebody shoulda pulled the curtains. Heck, there's bars on the window.

Red squinted at the late-evening sun shining in through the small window above his bed. Turning his head slightly to the left, he stared in surprise at three other cots in the room. Two of them held sleeping men, the other, stripped of linen, held a rolled-up mattress tied with cord.

"What the devil gives here?" he muttered aloud, straining to push himself to a sitting position.

"Hold it there, sonny. You're not going anywhere. Just settle yourself down. I'm glad to see you're finally awake. I was beginning to believe you planned to lie there without blinking for the rest of your life."

A tall, round man, dressed in a once-white coat, got up from a desk near a door and lumbered across the room to stand beside Red's bed. "I'm Big Doc, sonny. You just take it easy now. You've been out of it for more than a week. You're bound to be weak as a kitten. Just settle yourself back down on that pillow, and I'll get you some broth or something from the kitchen."

"Wait—wait a minute. What do you mean, I've been out for more than a week? What in the heck is this place?"

"You've been lying there like a bump on a log for ten days—soon be eleven. You're in the infirmary at Yuma. Old Pritchard was cussin' and fussin' when he got you here. He thought for sure you'd died on him. He came running in here yelling like a wild Indian for me to come outside and check if you were dead or not."

Big Doc shook his head. "I saw where that wound on your head was sewn up as neat as a pin. The doctor who tended you had a sure hand. I took the stitches out. That wound was in a bad place, but it's healing fine, and your hair will grow back pretty soon. Your doctor should have made you stay flat in bed until your head stopped hurting. You had a serious concussion."

The physician shrugged. "I don't know just what happened to you, but that blow to the back of your head bruised your brain, son. Mother Nature demands time for healing after something like that. When you got to stirring around too much to give yourself time to heal, she just put you down to give that hurt the chance to heal itself."

"My head stopped hurting." Red pushed himself up from the pillow to rub the back of his head.

"That's good news. Lie back down now, and I'm gonna get you something to eat. We've been spooning some water and broth down your throat, but you'll need something more to help you get some strength back."

The doctor turned toward the door. Just before he reached it, he turned to look back at Red. "If anybody else comes into this room, you close your eyes and lie still. It'll take a few days for you to be fit to move to a cell. If everybody knows you're awake, they might push me to discharge you too soon."

I'm in Yuma, but I'm in the infirmary. I almost feel like my head is empty. At least it doesn't hurt anymore. The cut is plumb healed up, and my hair's growing back—I can feel the stubble. But I still feel sleepy.

When Red woke again, it was morning, and the man called Big Doc was standing beside his cot.

"Let me get this extra pillow under your head, Thornton, so you can raise yourself up a little. Here's a cup of broth. It's made from boiled jerky, so it'll help you get your strength back. Can you hold it?"

Red closed both hands around the cup, raised it to his lips, and sipped. "It sure is salty."

"That'll help you. Drink it up, and go back to sleep. I'll try to get you another cup every hour or two. You'll be able to eat regular food in a day or two."

"Thanks, Doc. I'm obliged to you."

"Give me the cup. You slide back down now and rest. I'll be back in a few hours. Remember what I told you. At least try to sleep most of the day. Every night I come on duty right after supper and stay until after breakfast. If we can get you through until tomorrow night before anybody finds out, you'll be better able to officially 'wake up.' "

Turning away and walking softly for such a large man, the physician went back to his desk, gathered up a book and writing pad, and left the room, closing the door softly behind him.

Red looked around the room again as he settled back against the pillow. The other two men were stirring. The one in the nearest cot was awake. His face turned toward Red, and his blue eyes stared at him.

"Hello. My name is Red Thornton." Red managed a smile as he whispered.

"I see you did finally wake up. I'm Fitch Welton. That other fella over there is James Bell. We been betting you never would wake up."

"I sure am glad you were wrong."

"You got that right. What the heck happened to you, anyway?"

"A fella pushed me, and I fell against some stone steps. It knocked me out, and I was sort of befuddled before I was sent here. That fella called Big Doc said I passed out in the prison wagon when Pritchard was bringing me down from Gila Bend."

"That's what we heard. You been lying there still as a mouse for more'n a week. I was plain out amazed when I heard you and Big Doc whispering this morning."

"Big Doc seems like a nice guy."

"He is, but he's got to sorta hide it around here. The new warden ain't as bad as the old one, but he's still a stickler for rules. Big Doc seems to make up his own rules as far as the infirmary goes. The day doc will get here in a few minutes. He ain't no real doctor like the other fella. He's all right, though, if you don't give him no trouble. He's got his own problems."

"I'm too weak to give anybody any trouble."

"That'll go away fast enough—soon's you get to moving again."

"I'm always so sleepy. I hope that goes away soon."

"Go back to sleep, then. I reckon I'll probably be leaving here tomorrow or the next day. I had me a nasty kind of grippe or ague, but I'm over it now. I've just been getting all the rest they'd allow me."

Red turned his head and drifted back to sleep, wondering what prison would be like when he left the infirmary.

Fitch Welton was gone when he woke up.

With Big Doc's help, Red managed to stay in the infirmary for another week. He was on his feet the second night and, urged by Big Doc, walked up and down the room for a longer time each night, until he was feeling stronger every day.

"What did they do with my clothes, Doc? I feel a little exposed walking around in this nightgown."

"They'll give you some clothes when you go back into the regular part of the prison, son. They take everybody's personal things. They dump them into a croker sack and put them away somewhere. You'll get them back when you leave here—if you ever do."

Near the end of the week, Red begged a sheet of paper and wrote a letter to his father and Chief Billy, telling them he arrived at the prison without problems, felt fine, and was being well treated. Big Doc agreed to mail it for him.

It was almost dark when Big Doc entered the room. He walked directly to where Red sat on his cot, reading an old newspaper.

"Well, Thornton, I've got my orders. You're going into the general population tomorrow. I managed to put the warden off two extra days, but there's no way I can convince him you're not able to do light work. He agreed not to put you to doing anything heavy for another week. That's the best I can do for you."

"You probably saved my life, Doc, and I thank you. I don't know how I could ever repay you, but I will if I ever can."

"I see you don't have but five years, Thornton. Keep your head down, and do what you're told. You'll make it through."

"I plan on it, Doc." Red held out his hand. "Good-bye."

Dear Red,

It's good to hear you can work with the guards in that place. I feared you'd get some sadistic devil who'd make your life as miserable as he possibly could. I'm sure the work and life are hard enough without having to face that.

Winter stays open up here so far. We had a little trouble with a bear, but that wild stallion you call Pitch and the dogs drove him up close to the cabin, and Chief Billy shot him. He's working on the skin—says he's going to make me another robe for my bunk. I think it might be too heavy to sleep under, though.

Your mares are fine. Pitch lets us handle them some, but he keeps a close eye on us. We've used this good weather to fence in some more pasture to the east of the barn. There's a few rocks sticking out of the ground here and there, but the grass is good.

We built another shelter for the horses. We were getting along so good with the work that Billy and I rechinked the spaces between the logs in the cabin and overlaid the floor with deer hides and wolf skins. We've had no trouble keeping warm. Billy cut enough logs to keep the fire going two winters, and we've got plenty of food.

I reckon this might be the last letter we'll get out until the spring thaw. Billy says he'll make this his last trip down the mountain before the snow. It seems, according to him, we're in for a big storm in a few days. He claims it's his Indian medicine telling him. He's leaving for town early tomorrow

*and will get back here late. He says we'll be
snowed in after that 'til spring.*

*We're snug, though, and so are the horses. We
haven't seen anybody since the cold weather started.
Billy takes a turn around every day to check for
tracks, but he's not seen a thing. He cut three big
stacks of hay for the horses. We made a stone boat,
and he ties a big bundle of hay on it and drags the
sled behind that dun horse of his. We've got it
piled up near the barn with the top covered by a
tarp to keep the weather off.*

*Don't you worry about us—or your stock either.
We're fine, and we'll get another letter out as soon
as we can. Let me hear from you soon.*

> *As Always,*
> *Dad and Chief Billy*

*I couldn't help but think it almost sounded like those
two old rascals were making a game out of this. I figure there's a lot going on up there that didn't make it
into this letter. They always had a way of doing that to
me. A body might think I was still ten years old.*

*I've kinda soft-pedaled things a bit from this end too,
I guess. I don't reckon I have much room to criticize
Dad and Billy for making light of their troubles. There's
nothing any one of us can do to help the other, so what
the heck?*

*I have to admit I was scared witless when I got out of
that infirmary. I was lucky, though. I happened to get*

into the main part of the prison in the middle of one of their "sale" days.

It was about the strangest experience I ever expect to have.

Red had stepped through the gate to see a bunch of prisoners lined up along one side of the yard. Three or four dressed-up fellows were standing in front of them, waving their arms and yelling out bids.

He was confused at first. There didn't seem to be anything for the men to be bidding on. As he watched, it finally came though—they were bidding on the men lined up in front of them.

One of the guards saw Red's shocked face and came over to explain. "They don't really 'sell' the men, Thornton—slavery's outlawed in the Territory—they only sell the convicts' labor. The good thing about the whole deal is, we can sell the convict labor over and over, every year, as long as the men are in the prison."

Red shuddered. The same guard grabbed his shoulder with one hand and shoved him over to join another group of prisoners. Some of those men looked scared half to death, and some just looked bored. He noticed they were all burned as brown as drovers from being out in the sun.

Red stumbled as he joined the group and bumped up against one big fellow. The man spun around like he was ready to fight, but when he got a good look at Red's face, he waved a hand and sorta smirked.

It was Fitch Welton, the prisoner from the infirmary. He looked so serious, Red couldn't rightly tell if the man would be friendly or not for a minute, but he finally got up enough nerve up to ask him to explain what was happening.

Fitch looked at Red like he was a complete fool and turned back to watch the men still calling out bids. Red thought at first that Fitch was going to ignore him, but with his face turned away, Welton muttered under his breath.

"Them there fellas is road contractors. They come in here every few months and buy themselves a couple hundred hands to do the road repair work they've got contracts for."

Welton subtly pointed with his chin. "That big fella over on the right—the one with the black jacket on—he goes by the name of Jeff Landry. He's got a contract to work the washes out of the road going west out of here. I ain't plumb sure where it goes."

Fitch scratched one ear and continued. "I worked for him the last round before that spell of grippe put me in the infirmary, and his was the best camp I ever been in. He feeds good and don't allow his guards to whip on the men. I'm hoping he gets first pick today. If he does, I figure he'll sure pick me, 'cause he knows I'm a right smart worker."

When Welton said that, my head started in to hurting again. Must be just plain nerves. Or the idea of being sold. Now, that's out and out unsettling.

The contractor named Jeff Landry won the bidding. He and the other bidders went outside the prison walls and stood on either side of the open gate. The guards yelled for the prisoners to get into line and start walking toward the gate.

Red decided that since all he knew about the situation was what Fitch Welton told him, his best bet was to watch Welton and do what he did. Fitch stepped out briskly, and Red stayed close behind him. When the line got close to the gate, Jeff Landry and a taller man Red found out later was Landry's foreman were counting off men as they came out.

Some of the men in line ahead of Welton and Red were stooped over and sick looking. One even walked with a cane. There were two really short ones who stuck close together. When Red finally got a good look at their faces, he was amazed to see that they were mere boys. They couldn't be more than ten or twelve years old. Landry didn't take any notice. He kept counting, and everybody kept moving.

Fitch Welton and Red walked through the gate with about six other men who looked strong and healthy. When they saw the group, Landry and his man seemed to perk up a little. Red wasn't quite as tall as Welton or as big, but he had thick shoulders and arms, and it was easy to see he was used to hard work.

Landry kept waving the men through the gate, and two more fellows with Greener coach guns signaled for them to climb into one of seven wagons lined up in the shade of the prison wall.

Each wagon bed was made of rough boards with

some straw piled around, but it had an iron cage over it. It was sort of makeshift. Red figured this one was probably homemade, but it worked the same as the prison wagon he rode when Pritchard brought him to Yuma from Gila Bend. Red climbed into the nearest wagon and found a seat along the side, so he wouldn't have to ride backward.

I didn't want to get to feeling like puking again like I did on the stage.

The road work was hard, and it was bad for Red at first, but according to Welton, it could have been ten times worse. He claimed working for Landry was the best detail the prisoners could get.

When Landry found out that Red could write and figure, he made him a sort of deputy foreman. His job was to carry the scale drawings and maps they needed to constantly refer to. He kept records of work hours for Landry's crew as well.

Another thing Landry did was encourage the men in his crew by letting them work one day a week for wages if they really put their backs into it for him the rest of the week. Welton and Red managed to get one day on wages every single week.

They both figured that if everything went right, they would at least leave Yuma with a little money in their pockets. Welton had about the same time left as Red would serve—four more years on a ten-year sentence for robbing a stage.

It was a rule that everyone had to go back into the main prison about once a month. The men all lined up in the yard to be counted by the head guard. Then they went to the infirmary, and the day doctor checked them over. He was usually either drunk or on laudanum or something—Red and Fitch always laughed about it.

I don't really know why they bother to check us. It may just be a habit they can't break. I've never seen anybody get taken off the crew because he was sick.

After every man was checked over, they went to the dining room to eat a meal. It was usually beef and beans with tortillas—sometimes some greens boiled with fatback were added—but most of the men appreciated the chance to eat at a table, whatever was served.

Landry fed good, like Welton told me that day in the yard, but eating squatting by the fire or sitting on a box with a tin plate on your knees gets old.

The men stayed in the main prison yard for a few hours after they ate, then piled back into the wagons and went back to the road camp. Out there, they lived four or sometimes five to a tent, spreading their blankets on the ground to sleep.

Nobody ever tried to run away from Landry's camp though. It would be foolish, if not plain suicidal, to try such a thing out in the open like it was. There was no drinking water to speak of anywhere around. That was probably the main reason nobody tried to run away.

Plenty of men were sent back to the prison, though. The camp guards assigned work according to what a man was capable of doing, but they didn't show much patience if a man didn't work hard enough. Wagons left with five or six men at a time sitting in the cage behind the driver and a guard with a shotgun turned around on the seat, watching them.

Stretching out on his cot, Red read his father's letter again. It hardly seemed possible, but almost three years had slipped away since he'd been in Yuma, and it would soon be winter again. He'd gotten at least one letter from his father for every month he was in prison, although sometimes they came two or three at once. This letter was the most hopeful sounding yet.

Dad and Billy sound like they're still afraid Gilbert Patten and his men will try to run off some of our stock. For all I know, they mighta tried. I'm pretty sure I wouldn't hear about it in a letter if they did. I know if those two old devils killed enough wolves and other varmints to make that carpet for that big cabin of Billy's, they've had their hands full protecting the stock.

If they do get snowed in again, and I reckon they will, all I can do is worry until the weather opens up. It could be as late as next April before they can get to town again.

Billy could snowshoe down the mountain and back if he was by himself, but I guess he figures he'd better not leave Dad all that time. He could get hurt too, and that would leave Dad up there with no help.

Dear Son,

Well, we made it through again. You've got five more fillies and two colts born to your mares. Every single one of them looks exactly like that devilish Pitch of yours. Billy says we have to get our hands on these babies every day, so they won't grow up mean like their papa.

Me and Billy had us a little bit of a set-to with some fellas the day before yesterday. There were three of them altogether. I didn't know any of them for sure, but one sat his horse an awful lot like that sorry Wes Lane.

Two of them, the ones that were strangers to me, rode up to the cabin, bold as brass, and the other one—the one I thought was Wes—sat his horse over by that low crag with the crooked pine on top.

I stepped out onto the front stoop to talk to the men.

About the time I said howdy, Billy happened to see sunlight wink off a rifle the man over on the crag was holding. He had his gun up to his shoulder and was drawing a bead on me. Billy shot him.

When I heard Billy's gun, I drew on the other two and faced them down.

Those two fellas held their hands up over their heads and backed their horses well away from me, then turned and rode out of there.

I'm still not exactly sure what the deal was sup-

posed to be. We never knew the true identity of the man Billy shot. Those two fellas packed him away.

We could see them in the distance. The man still sat his saddle, but he lay up over the horn like he was bad hurt. We finally figured it didn't really matter much who the low-down sucker was, anyway.

We keep closer watch now. Billy says it was probably Wes or maybe Gilbert Patten making sure I don't claim your mother's share of the White Willow Ranch when his daddy dies.

Billy thinks one of the men who came into the yard used to work over to White Willow. He wore a hat Billy claimed he recognized. He also remembers seeing the other one in the Red Wheel, drinking with Patten and his bunch.

Take care, son. Me and Billy miss you something fierce, but we're watchful.

Love Always,
Dad and Billy.

The clanging of a metal rod slammed against the iron frying pan hanging from the ridgepole of the cookshack wakened the camp. Red sat up instantly, throwing his blankets aside to pull on his heavy shoes. He wanted to shave and clean up before chow and knew he'd have to hurry, or somebody else would beat him to the water barrel.

Grabbing his soap and a clean shirt, he rushed out of the tent. No one was in sight. First to the barrel, he dipped icy water into a semiclean bucket and began to soap his face. The guard standing near the barrel grinned as he watched Red repeatedly rub his shaving brush over his bar of yellow soap and apply the skimpy lather to his face.

"I don't see why you bother, Thornton. I sharpened the razor last night, but even so, it's got to be torture to try to shave in that cold water."

"I know. It makes me feel better to be clean, though."

"Well, better you than me. Here's the razor. You know I have to stand here and watch you 'til you finish."

"That's all right by me. I've been doing this at least twice a week for almost three years. I don't mind."

Scraping his whiskers away as cleanly as possible with cold water and insufficient lather, Red wished for a mirror. He hadn't seen his likeness since he left home to meet Wes that awful day three years before.

I wonder what I'll look like when I get out of here. I've maybe got two more years to go, my face'll surely be sun-roughened like Welton's and the rest of the prisoners'.

When he finished shaving and handed the razor back to the guard, he soaped a rag and shuddered with cold as he bathed the upper part of his body. When he finished drying off, he pulled on the clean shirt and tucked it into his heavy cord trousers. Still shivering, he removed one heavy shoe at a time and washed his feet.

"Get out of the way, Thornton. You're clean enough."

Red turned to wave acknowledgment of an approaching prisoner. The man carried a clean shirt, a semiclean sacking towel, and another bar of the coarse yellow soap.

"It felt so chilly, I thought I'd find a skim of ice in the water barrel this morning, but I guess we'll not freeze, even if it does feel like it," Red said to the man.

"It's a good thing you decided to prettify yourself this morning, boy. I seen Landry ride the cage into camp a few minutes ago. I figure something's up. That's why I decided to put on a clean shirt," the fellow replied.

Chapter Five

Looking up as he finished drying his feet on the piece of once-white feed sacking, Red noticed snow still lying on the upper reaches of the larger mountains. He wondered if the snow had finished melting around Billy's place. The sun would start to beat down in a few hours and make it almost as hot as summer in the middle of the day, but it was still fairly cold this early in the morning.

One of the guards called out, "Hey, Thornton. Come over here."

Startled, Red pulled his plaid blanket jacket over his gray prison-issue shirt and started walking toward the man.

What in Sam Hill does he want? Landry's standing

over there with him. I know I haven't broken any camp rules, and I was part of the crew that went over to the prison last week, so it can't be that.

A shiver of fear went down Red's back. A little resentful because of how uncomfortable the summons made him feel, he kept his face expressionless as he walked deliberately up to the group of guards gathered around Jeff Landry.

"You come with me, Thornton," Landry said. "I'm riding guard on a punishment wagon over to the prison. I got a message from the warden last night. He wants to see you about something, pronto."

Red nodded without speaking and followed Landry to the wagon. His thoughts swirled dizzily as he climbed through the narrow door and found a seat in one of the back corners.

I'd like to know what the heck is going on. I know I haven't broken any rules, and it hasn't been a month since I heard Landry raving to one of the assistant wardens about how much help I am to him by keeping track of all the prisoners' work hours.

Oh, Lord. I hope everything is all right at home.

When they arrived in the prison yard, Landry jumped down from the wagon seat and motioned for Red to follow him into the stone building. He opened the door under a sign saying WARDEN and stepped into a room divided front to back by a long counter.

"You wait out here, Thornton. I'll let Warden Howe

know you're here to see him." Lowry pointed to a bench along the front wall as he left the room to disappear down a narrow hallway to the right.

This is a puzzle. Something's happened to Dad—that has to be it. There's nothing else it could be—it must be Dad. I know I haven't broken any rules.

I hope to goodness they're not planning to move me someplace else to work. It's bad enough to be here at all, but I sure don't want to be moved someplace worse than where I am.

It's Dad, though. It's bound to be Dad.

He dropped his head back against the wall and closed his eyes.

Hearing a sound, he looked up to see a tall, heavyset man dressed in a guard's uniform push open the front door and step into the room. He was whistling.

When the guard saw Red, he stopped suddenly and bellowed, "What do you think you're doing in this office, convict?"

Red stayed where he was, looked up at the man, and started to answer. "I'm waiting—"

"What's the matter with you—don't you know nothing? Stand up when you talk to me."

Moving closer, the guard stood toe-to-toe with Red when he got to his feet.

"That's better. Now let's hear it—what's your name, and what the devil are you doing in here?"

"I came in here with Mr. Landry. He said I should wait here. He's in the warden's office."

"Well, you stand over there by the wall. You should know better than to lounge around like that. Don't you be leaning against the wall, either. I swear, every one of you cons is eaten up with laziness."

A door slammed, and Landry emerged from the hallway.

Another man was right behind him. "What in the world is all the shouting about out here, Perkins?" the man asked in a low voice.

"Warden Howe, when I came into the office a minute ago, this here convict was taking his ease over there on the bench. I was just getting him straightened out until I could find out how come he's sitting around in here with no shackles on and no guard with him or nothing."

"Perkins, it's not your problem. Mr. Thornton is here to see me. I'll take care of everything. You go along and see to your own work."

His face red, the guard walked behind the counter and took a chair. He stared angrily at Red.

Warden Howe turned to Red. "Come into my office, Thornton. I want to read you part of a letter and give you some papers."

Red felt the blood leave his face and his stomach lurch. Fear shook his entire body.

I was right. Something's happened to Dad. I knew it.

When they reached his office, Howe walked behind a polished wooden desk and sat down. Looking up at the two men, he said, "Take a seat, Thornton. You too,

Landry. This won't take a minute. I'll just read you the pertinent part of Judge Sellers' letter to me."

Warden Howe cleared his throat. "The judge says here in the second paragraph, *Rufus Thornton has served almost three years of a three- to five-year sentence, and I understand he has been an exemplary inmate. I'd be obliged if you would free the man as soon as possible and make sure he can return to his home at Acorn Creek.*"

Stunned, Red stared from Warden Howe to Landry's smiling face. When he could control his voice, he managed to ask, "Dad's all right, then? This has nothing to do with my dad? You—you mean I—I—you mean it's over? I can go home?"

"It's true, Thornton. This is unusual—I'll give you that—but it's absolutely true. I know Judge Matthew L. Sellers to be a harsh man. I've known the old devil for years. I've gotten several letters from him asking me to keep a prisoner longer than his formal sentence for various reasons, but this is a new one on me."

Howe shook his head. "When I received this letter, I contacted Mr. Landry here, and he gave you a superior recommendation, so I went ahead and had your release papers prepared for you so I could put them into your hands myself. If anybody should challenge you after you leave, they're all you need. As of this minute, Thornton, you're a free man."

Landry slapped Red's shoulder and held out a small leather pouch. "I've got something here you'll need,

Thornton. It's your salary-day pay. You've accumulated almost one hundred dollars. I'm going to miss your help on the job."

Warden Howe came around the desk and held out his right hand. "Thornton, I got the idea from Judge Sellers' letter that he's grown doubtful of your guilt for some reason or other."

Red took the man's hand and shook his head as he heard the question in Howe's voice. "I know you hear this a lot, sir, but I'm not guilty of Johnny Yates' murder. I truly believe Judge Sellers always knew I wasn't guilty."

Howe stared at Red for a moment, then shook his head. "Sellers is a slick old bird—I'll give you that—but it's hard for me to believe he'd send you down here for five years without proof of your guilt."

"I guess he and the jury heard enough of what sounded like proof, Warden Howe, but I didn't shoot the man, and one of these days I'll find a way to prove I didn't shoot him."

"If that's the case, I understand how you must feel, Thornton. But don't you spend time dwelling on it. You're much more fortunate than most ex-convicts. You've got people behind you, a little bit of money, and you're young. Don't spend your time and energy looking back. Look ahead, and make a good life for yourself."

"Thank you, Warden Howe. I'll remember that."

"Landry here can show you where to go to get your personal things and change clothes. You can ride back up to Gila Bend with Pritchard. He's waiting for you just outside the gate."

Surprised, Red asked. "Well, now, are you sure Pritchard'll take me? From what I can remember, he acted pretty unfriendly when he put me into that cage at Gila Bend three years ago."

"It's all right, Thornton, I promise. Pritchard does hate a convict, but he doesn't hate anybody making the trip back. Once you're a free man, he'll treat you like a human being again. I guess he figures that when a man's released from here, he's paid his debt, and it's not up to him to try to draw interest after the fact."

Red's boots were so tight, he had to stomp hard to get them onto his feet, and his shoulders filled out the blue shirt and his jacket closely enough to make them feel snug. But he was so happy to hand the clerk his prison-issue clothes and heavy, thick-soled shoes, he hardly noticed.

When he'd finished dressing and turned in his prison-issued clothes, the clerk led him down a hallway to a door opening out to the yard. As soon as he stepped outside, he saw Pritchard standing near the gate.

Pritchard waved and called out, "Over here, Thornton. Come on. I got to be getting on the road."

My spine tingles as if someone is training a shotgun on me. This is amazing—almost unbelievable. It wouldn't surprise me to hear one of those guards yelling, "Stop, or I'll shoot!"

When he reached the gate, Red stopped to look back. He was the only person in the yard. The wagon that had brought him and Landry in from the camp was gone.

Turning his back on the buildings, he stepped through the gate onto the hard-packed dirt of the roadway.

"Climb up here beside me, son. I got to get this rig moving, or we'll be dark reaching our sleeping place."

Red climbed over the wheel and clambered aboard.

"Say, you ain't carrying a blasted thing. Didn't them fools even give you a blanket?" Pritchard said.

Red shook his head as he settled on the seat beside Pritchard with his back to the iron cage.

"Shucks a'mighty. It's a blame good thing it ain't totally freezing out here. You'll get cold, and that's a fact, but you won't die of it. I'll pull one of them rags outen the cage for you to use. I can flap it over the fire long enough to kill most of the fleas without setting it alight."

"Obliged," Red said.

Pritchard shook his head. "I got us plenty of grub, at least. You won't want for something in your belly."

"I'm obliged, Mr. Pritchard. Let me know if you want me to spell you at the reins."

"Nope. Nobody drives my teams but me, sonny. No offense to you. I'm sure you're good at driving and all, but these four matched bays are my pets, I guess you could say. They ain't used to nobody's hands on the leathers but mine."

"I understand. I think I'll just lean my head back and catch me some shut-eye while you drive, then."

"You go ahead, boy. I got to watch what I do for a few miles, anyway. This next stretch of road is rough as a cob."

I'm not sleepy, but I need to think. If I keep my eyes closed, it's almost as good as being alone.

This is all crazy. Everything happened so fast, I'm having a hard time keeping up. Why in the world would Judge Sellers write to the warden and ask him to let me out early? There's something going on I can't figure out. I wonder if I'll ever find out what it is.

Chapter Six

Gila Bend was asleep when Pritchard's wagon rattled to a stop in front of a tall adobe building. The front door stood open, and Red could see lights flickering in several windows on the second floor.

"It's like I done told you, Thornton. This here cantina is the only place in this town that'll take in any of the ex-cons I bring in from Yuma. The people what run the boardinghouse, the store, and the saloon are glad enough to take your money iffen you happen to have any, but they just plain don't want you around. I ain't figured out yet whether they're born mean and can't help it, or if they might be afraid of you men."

Pritchard shrugged and scratched his chin. "Either way, my advice to you is, don't even go to the store unless you plumb got to. Old Chavez'll rent you a bed and

77

feed you cheap. The food ain't bad either, and his beds is always clean.

"You got to wait around here two days for the stage that runs north to Acorn Creek. It's easy for somebody like you to get into trouble in this stinking burg. You don't have to do anything much to cause it either."

"Why's that?" Red asked.

"It's like they all want you to go back down to Yuma. Like they can't believe a man can pay his debt and come outta there clean. I think they're just a bunch of low-down suckers that are wicked clear through."

"I'll stay close to the cantina, Mr. Pritchard. All in the world I want is to get back home where I belong. I'm not gonna bother anybody."

"Well, I ain't fooling you none about this town, son. You got to be careful. I done took more than one poor boy back down that miserable road to Yuma prison 'cause he had trouble with somebody in this sorry town.

"If you go to the store or anywhere else, the sheriff will be watching and hoping to get something on you so he can throw you into his jail. The town judge will send you back to Yuma for anything—just anything."

"I'm obliged, sir—for the ride and the advice. I'll keep my head down and get out of here early Thursday on the stage."

Pritchard shook Red's hand and clambered back up behind the horses.

Red stood still. No one else was on the street. Pritchard

turned his horses off to the right and moved out of sight.

This is the first time I've really been alone in almost three years. It's hard to take in. I can stand right here as long as I want or go inside when I want without asking leave of anybody.

It's hard to take in.

With a small smile, Red finally turned to step through the open doorway of the cantina. A heavyset man with a black mustache, obviously a Mexican, sat on a stool behind the counter. He spoke English with only a slight accent.

"Good morning, stranger. Did I see you step down from Señor Pritchard's prison wagon?"

"Yes," Red said, his back stiffening a little as he walked up to the counter. "My name is Thornton. Mr. Pritchard said you'd provide me room and board until the stage leaves going north."

"Do you have money, Señor Thornton?"

"I do."

"That is a good thing for you, and also it is a good thing for me. I would not turn you away if you had no money, but it is a good thing for you to have some money."

"I can certainly agree with you on that. How much?"

"The stage comes through early Thursday morning. You will be here two nights. Can you give me two dollars?"

"I can, and it seems more than fair."

"It is to help the next man. My nephew is in Yuma. He may be the next man who comes through. I always ask for two dollars from those who have money so I can help the man who comes with nothing."

"You've got a good point there, my friend. I'd kinda like to add a couple more dollars to the two you asked for. I wouldn't want to hit a town that hates ex-convicts with no money in my pocket."

"You have a good heart, Señor Thornton. I thank you, and I will take your money. It will be used for the next man who comes with no money."

Chavez didn't get down from his stool but waved his hand to his left and said, "You go up the stairs over there to the second floor. Your room is the first door on the right-hand side. The water pitcher is full, and you will find a clean towel hanging beside it. Hot food will be ready as soon as you can wash the dust off your face.

"If you want to buy things from the store, make a list, and I will make the purchases for you. It is best you stay inside this building until it is time for the stage to leave."

The stage rattled across the bridge at Acorn Creek and rolled to a stop in front of the hotel. The sweating horses hung their heads and stood quietly, clearly grateful for the respite.

Red stepped down into the dusty street and hesitated a moment to look at the group of men lounging on the hotel porch. When he started to walk across the street to the hotel, a short man in a yellow shirt gasped out loud and jumped out of his chair to stare his way. After a moment he turned to run around the side of the building. Three other men stayed in their chairs but leaned forward to stare at Red.

Ignoring the gawkers, Red turned back to wave a hand to the stage driver and headed for the hotel. Mounting the steps, he walked across the porch to go inside. The lobby was empty. Moving to the desk, he spun the ledger around and wrote his name, then slapped the bell.

Curly Benton stuck his bald head out of the office to yell, "Grab yourself a key off the rack, and leave a dollar on the desk."

"What the Sam Hill?" Red muttered.

When Benton saw that it was Red standing at the counter, he came rushing out of the office, a big smile on his face. "Is that you, Red?"

"You've got me, Curly. I need a room for one night, and then I'm off to Heard's Mountain to find my dad and Chief Billy."

"Well, by jinks, it's some kinda good to see you standing there, boy—here's my hand. I'm proud to be the first one to welcome you home."

"That's good of you, Curly. I'm not a bit sure the rest of the town will feel that way about it."

"I don't know about that, Red. I do know a lot of people are beginning to wonder about Wes Lane and his doings. Some folks have started to think maybe it's possible he did lie about your shooting poor old Johnny Yates."

"That so?" Red asked quietly.

Curly nodded vigorously. "Say, aren't you getting here some early? I thought Judge Sellers gave you five years in Yuma."

"You're right about that, Curly. The judge gave me a three- to five-year sentence. But five years was the maximum, and I got some time off for good behavior. It's hard for me to believe, but I've been gone three years this month."

The doors of the hotel flew open, and Sheriff Logan rushed through, a concerned look on his face. "What are you doing here, Red?" he asked breathlessly.

"Calm yourself, Sheriff. I got properly released from Yuma, and I've got the papers to prove it right here."

Red pulled a long envelope out of a pocket on the side of his bundle and held it out to Logan.

Deputy Leon Jackson came through the door and stood just behind Sheriff Logan, his little pig eyes glaring pure malice at Red, his hand on the grip of his pistol.

"Well, I'll be a cross-eyed mule," Sheriff Logan said. "They let you outa that place at three years, less a little extra time for good behavior. That's about the most surprisingest thing I've ever heard tell of."

The sheriff shrugged and said, "You sure are a lucky man, Thornton. Most men what get sent to Yuma serve every single day of their sentence, and then those people down there find a way to give 'em a few extra days for good measure."

Red stared back at Leon's angry-looking expression for a minute, then turned his eyes to meet Logan's. "I'm not exactly sure I'm 'lucky,' Logan. I've lost almost three years of my life. Dad and Chief Billy Two Horses are up there on the mountain trying to save my horses from Patten's thieves, and my cattle are scattered to Hades and gone. On top of that, most people in my hometown believe I'm a low-down drunken murderer. That doesn't sound like a lot of 'luck' to me."

Logan pushed his hat back and shook his head. "I guess you're right at that, Thornton. I can't help with your horses or cattle, but me and Leon will pass the word around town about your release. Folks'll get over this soon enough.

"I will tell you this, Red. You probably should stay out of town as much as you can for a few weeks—just until folks get used to the idea."

"Sheriff, I've told you from the very first minute of this fandango, I did not kill Johnny Yates. I'm not about to sneak around and hide in my own hometown because you and most of the people in this town choose to believe a lie."

Leon Jackson stepped forward to stand beside Sheriff Logan. "You've been warned, Thornton. Me and a lot of other people in this town thought a lot of Johnny Yates. He helped your granddads start this here town.

You need to know this—you just plain ain't welcome in Acorn Creek."

Red raised his voice as he looked down at the deputy. "Leon, you don't run this town. Sheriff Logan does. And as long as I don't break the law, you don't run me—so back off."

Sheriff Logan turned to shove Leon with one hand. "Shut your mouth, Leon. For heaven's sake. Didn't you hear anything I said? Red's served his time. He's just like anybody else in town now. I'm going to make it my business to see he's treated right. That means by you and everybody else. Do you understand me?"

Without answering and still looking angry, Leon turned away from the sheriff and left the hotel, slamming the door behind him.

"He's not gonna be the only one, Red. You've got to face it. You'll have to hold on to your temper for a while. Folks'll get over it after a bit if you give them a chance."

Red didn't answer for a long moment, staring after Leon. He finally raised his head, looked into Sheriff Logan's eyes, and said in a bitter voice, "I'm on my way out of town first thing in the morning, Logan. I'll not bother you or the people of this town any more than I have to."

Not waiting for an answer, Red picked up his carpetbag, turned his back on Logan, and climbed the stairs to find his room.

Chapter Seven

The sun was barely up when Red woke the next morning. He shaved in tepid water and dressed quickly, pulling on his jacket as he left the room to clatter down the stairs.

Willie Martin, who ran the desk during the day, stared without speaking when he stopped to return his room key. Two older men standing on the porch made a big production of showing him their backs when he stepped out of the hotel door.

The devil with them. I'll not stay in town long enough to bother about them or anybody else.

Without stopping for breakfast, Red headed straight to the livery. The big front doors of the stable stood open. When he stuck his head into the office, Burt Glassner stood up, grinning, and held out his hand.

"By jiggers, boy, it's good to see you. I heard talk around town earlier this morning that you were back home. I call that a bit of all right."

"It's good of you to say so, Burt. Some folks I've seen so far musta been kin to Johnny Yates by the way they take on. They all sure believe I shot him."

"Well, it sure did look bad on you, Red, and all of them fellas don't know you like I do. I know if you'da shot Johnny like they said you did, you'da owned up to it, and you'da had a good reason for it."

"Tell me a little about what's been happening around town, Burt. Do you ever see Wes Lane?"

"That four-flusher! He run off with that Becky Mc-Clain girl, then dumped her off on Patten. I don't know how true it is, but some say he took up with some half-Injun girl from up north somewhere. His pa completely disowned him before he died."

"Wait a minute—you mean to say Major Lane is dead?"

"That's the gospel truth, Red, and it's a mystery. I'll tell you what all I know about it. Major Lane come to town one day back in the winter. I misremember what day it was, but I know he did come in, because he left his horse here. He had that Jack Dolman with him— stuck to him like glue.

"He went over to that lawyer, Ben Seymour's, office. He stayed in there near half the day. About mid-afternoon Major Lane and Seymour came out of the office together and went over to the courthouse.

"I don't know just where Jack Dolman got to—he wasn't with them. After a few minutes Lane came back here to get his horse, and I watched him head on out of town by himself. Didn't say nothing to me, of course. Lane never spoke to people like me.

"The next day, about noontime, one of Major Lane's hands rode in and got the sheriff. Logan came back late in the evening with Lane laid up in a wagon on a pile of straw. He'd been shot to doll rags. Doc Bailey worked over him, but he died later on that night."

"Did they find out who shot him?"

"Nobody knows for sure, but his old ranch hands all claim it was Gil Patten and some of his bunch.

"Anyway, Patten and a bunch of hard cases took over White Willow Ranch. They ran all the old hands off the place. A couple of Patten's men come into town for supplies now and agin, but nobody knows 'em, and nobody ever sees Wes or Gilbert Patten.

"Everybody around here does a lot of talking and thinking about what it all means, but nobody knows anything at all for sure."

"Thanks for telling me all that, Burt. I can't hardly believe it. By the way, have you seen Chief Billy or my dad recently?

"Not since the snow started melting."

"I'll be riding then. That is—if you'll lend me a horse."

"Take that steel dust in the first stall to the left. He

ain't in the class of that black of yours, but he'll take you up the mountain."

Red could feel hard eyes staring at him when he passed a group of men standing on the porch of the Red Wheel.

Ignoring them, he tied the horse in front of the Mc-Clains' place and stepped inside, stopping at the door long enough for his eyes to grow accustomed to the dimness.

A tall young woman came out of the kitchen and put plates in front of an elderly couple sitting near the back of the dining room. She turned and stopped what she was doing to stare at Red.

He gasped when he recognized her.

I can hardly believe what I see. It's Jeannie McClain. She looks about a foot taller than I remember—and all grown up.

Jeannie's dark hair was braided and pinned around her head. Her dress fitted everywhere.

Red continued to stare as the girl came closer. When she stood no more than a foot away, he finally found his voice.

"Jeannie—I—I came by to thank you for seeing I was fed decent when I was in jail. I'd like some breakfast now, if you don't mind my eating here."

Jeannie smiled, and her voice was low and soft. "I'm glad to see you back home, Red. Someone told me you came in last night. Sit down anywhere you'd like. I'll get you some breakfast and a cup of coffee."

Red watched in astonishment as she returned to the kitchen. Her hips swayed a little as she walked.

When Jeannie opened the door to the kitchen, a small boy so young he was still in a dress, toddled toward her and held up his arms. Picking the child up in her arms, she turned and shut the door.

Astonished, Red stared at the door, his mind blank. Finally he started thinking again and took a seat at the nearest table.

That can't be her child—that girl can't be more than sixteen, maybe seventeen, years old.

Jeannie came back into the dining room and closed the door behind her. Red watched carefully, but he didn't get another glimpse of the child. She placed his food and silverware on the table and turned to the counter to fill a cup with hot coffee.

Still puzzled, he tried to catch Jeannie's eye, but she kept her face turned away as she brought him his coffee.

"Enjoy your food while it's hot, Red. I have some things to do. I'll see you again soon."

Before Red could answer, she turned and went through the door to the kitchen and shut it behind her.

He was almost through eating when the door opened again. Jeannie came out, and Jeannie and Becky's father, Andrew McClain, followed her, turning to shut the door firmly behind him. He scowled as he walked past the table where Red was finishing his meal. The two men had never been more than passing friendly.

McClain looks different to me. I swear, I think he's stone-cold sober.

This has got to be the first time I ever saw him when he wasn't far along in drink. What in the world could have happened to explain that?

Red finished his coffee and left the money for his breakfast on the table. McClain was still standing behind the counter, staring at him with a mean look on his face, when he walked out of the door.

Untying the steel dust's reins, he led him back toward the livery. Burt met him at the main door of the barn.

"Burt, tell me something about the McClains. What's going on over there?"

"By thunder, Red. I shoulda told you before, but you didn't ask, and I was kinda afraid you'd think I was sticking my nose in where it didn't belong. I knowed you was kinda sweet on the older McClain girl."

"Who is the little boy over there?"

"I'd better tell you the whole tale, son. Come on in and sit. It's gonna take a while."

Burt led the way back to his office and dropped down into his chair.

"Take that chair in the corner, Red—knock those bridles over onto the floor. This is a hard story for a man to tell. I told you Wes Lane dumped the McClain girl over on Patten. Leastways, that's what everybody says happened.

"Well, late one evening, a fella nobody ever seen around here before drove a buggy up to the front of the McClain place. There was a woman sitting up on the seat beside him.

"My own boy seen it all and told me about it. The driver got out and helped the woman get down. The man went around to the back of the buggy, unstrapped a carpetbag, and walked over to set it down by the front door of the McClains' living quarters.

"The woman stood by the buggy until the man got back into the seat. He picked up the reins and drove on out past the church, like he was headed out of town.

"The woman didn't move for a while, just stood there and watched until the fella was out of sight. Finally she went over to the house, picked up the suitcase, and knocked on the door.

"My boy saw Jeannie McClain open the door and welcome the woman. She put her arms around her. They went into the house together and shut the door behind them. That's about all anybody knew about it for a couple of weeks. Then Doc Bailey started calling at the house almost every day.

"Of course, nobody ever got a word out of Doc Bailey except, "They need a doctor." Folks knew there was no use pestering him for information. That's all Doc Bailey ever will say about anybody, bless his old heart.

"After about two weeks of Doc's going over to the

McClain house every single day, some folks saw the reverend and Jed Martindale go in.

"You sure remember old Jed Martindale, don't you, Red? He's still the undertaker. Word got around town pretty quick that the oldest McClain girl—Rebecca, I think her real name is—had died in childbirth.

Red dropped his head into his hands to hide his tears. After a moment he raised his head and said in a strained voice, "Becky McClain, dead? That's a hard thing to think about, Burt."

"That's who the little boy is, Red. That Jeannie girl took her sister's baby, and she cares for him like he's her very own. She weren't but about fifteen or sixteen years old her own self when the boy was born.

"Martindale told me old Andrew McClain and that Reverend Sylvester wanted to take the baby to the church orphanage over to Palo Verde, but Jeannie stood there with the little one in her arms and plain out defied both of them. She works in that café every single day and still takes care of that boy.

"McClain quit drinking the day it happened. He used to stay soaked every day of his life—had done it ever since I knowed him. You remember that. The word is, he's never taken a drink since the night his girl died.

"I was told they buried the girl over to the McClains' home place. I hear it's somewhere near that little settlement name of Greensboro. The reverend wouldn't see to burying her in the churchyard, seeing as how she had that baby and wasn't even married to whoever the father was."

Red had dropped his head back into his hands again as he listened to Burt's recital. He raised his head to scowl and say, "That pompous old coot. He couldn't prove Becky and Wes didn't get married somewhere. He never gave anybody the benefit of the doubt in his life. Becky McClain was a good girl. If she went to the bad, it was Wes Lane's fault, not hers."

"Don't you get yourself riled up now, Red. Nobody faults that girl except that preacher and some of the old biddies around town that's lived so long, they've forgotten what life is really about.

"Poor little Jeannie has trouble herself sometimes. Some folks like to think she's bound to be bad too or she wouldn't be raising no baby without a husband."

"Thanks for telling me about it, Burt. I'm heading out to Chief Billy's place now. I want to talk to that lawyer about Major Lane, but I'll wait to talk to him until I get back to town again."

Red walked outside and mounted the steel dust. Clicking his tongue, he urged the horse to a trot, guiding him past the buildings and out onto the road. The sound of the horses' iron-shod hooves on the wooden bridge thundered through his head.

Becky McClain dead and Jeannie raising her child—it's hard to take it all in. I guess that sure explains the difference in old man McClain. I'd never seen him sober before.

I might need to have a talk with that reverend. I've got to find out where Wes Lane is too. If that's his boy, he should be taking care of him, not leaving him on that young girl to raise up by herself.

Chapter Eight

Patches of snow still lay here and there on the road when Red came within sight of the cabin. Slowing his horse to a walk, he examined the outbuildings, the paddock, and the fenced pasture. Smoke drifted up from the cabin's chimney.

He could see Pitch and five of the mares grazing in a low place where the snow was gone. Several foals nursed or danced around them.

Red stopped his horse about a hundred yards from the house and called out, "Hello the house!"

When he got no response, he called out again. "Hey, Billy. Hey, Dad. It's Red. Where the devil are you? I'm freezing out here."

The door of the cabin burst open, slamming back against the building. Billy Two Horses and Will

Thornton struggled to step through the door and onto the stoop at the same time, one trying to push the other out of the way.

"What in the blue blazes is this?" Billy yelled. "You didn't break out of prison, did you?"

Laughing at the expression on his father's face, Red dismounted and walked over to grab Will Thornton's shoulders with both hands.

"I served the minimum three years with some time off for good behavior. I'm free and done with Yuma prison for all time, Dad.

"I didn't get time to write and tell you I was on the way. The warden figured up my time and turned me loose the same day he got a letter from Judge Sellers telling him to let me go."

Billy Two Horses grabbed Red's right hand and pulled him toward the cabin. "Come on inside the house, you two. I ain't cutting enough wood to heat the whole dang-blasted countryside."

"Billy's right, son. Tie your horse to the rail there, and come on inside," Will said as he turned to re-enter the cabin.

Dropping the horse's reins so he would stand ground hitched, Red untied his bundle from behind the saddle and followed the two men inside.

Billy shut the door behind them and grabbed Red's hand again. "Sit down here at the table, boy. Tell me how you got them law dogs to leave you go so early. It ain't hardly been a full three years since they sent you down there."

"It's not really so early, Billy. The Judge said three to five years, and I kinda think Doc Bailey and Sheriff Logan spoke up for me, because the warden and the head guard down there treated me decent the whole time I was there.

"There's a regular system they've got of counting so many days off for every month a prisoner doesn't cause them any trouble and does his work with a will, and I got all they allow.

"When we were ready to leave for Yuma, right after the trial, Sheriff Logan told me something that meant a lot to me. He told me his own daddy had been locked up in an awful-sounding prison in a cave way up north one time in the War.

"He told Logan he made it through when a lot of men didn't 'cause he made up his mind to do whatever the guards asked him to do without any complaint.

"I thought about what he said on the way down to Yuma, and I decided I was going to do exactly what Logan's father did.

"I wanted to be home, right here with you two, to raise my horses and build our ranch back up. I decided I would do everything I could to get home as quickly as I could. I made up my mind to it, and here I am. It's as simple as that."

Billy made a sound almost like a horse snorting. "It

ain't nothing simple at all when you really think about it. That sorry Wes Lane and them fools down to Acorn Creek cost you near about three years of your life."

"I know, Billy, but I'm some kinda glad to be here now, and I want to forget all about it. I'd like to hear about how you and Dad got along while I was gone. I want to hear the real thing now, if you don't mind. Not the stuff you've been telling me in your letters."

Billy looked at him fiercely for a moment, but Red wasn't put off. "I saw Pitch and his ladies out there in the pasture as I was riding in. They sure look fine, but where are the yearlings and the two-year-olds?"

Billy turned his head and looked at Will.

Will made a sound like a groan and dropped his head onto the table. "I knew that would be the first thing you'd ask me about."

"What's wrong?"

"Red, I'm ashamed to tell you. We kept the young stock in the pasture above the barn. You can't see it from the way you came in. We thought if we set the dogs loose, nobody would bother the horses. Well, we heard the dogs baying one night—it musta been past midnight.

"By the time we got our boots on and got out there, the dogs lay on the ground dead—we heard the shots— and the young horses were gone. We followed the tracks as soon as it was light—at least, Billy did. We decided I ought to stay here to protect the other animals.

"The tracks led directly to White Willow Ranch. I

don't know if it was Wes who did it or not. I know he always envied you those horses. I heard Wes was out of the country and Gilbert Patten and his bunch had taken over the ranch, but I'm not sure what the full story is.

"Billy scouted the place and found out they've got your horses shut up in the big barn. They keep at least two men on guard all the time. Billy and I talked about stealing them back, but I don't know how we'd manage. I ain't the rider I used to be, and I figure if one of us was to get hurt—well, we'd be in a bad fix."

Red turned to Billy. "Did you go down and talk to the sheriff?"

"I ain't never had no use for that Logan. He's the sorriest excuse for a sheriff I ever heard tell of. I ain't about to ask him for no help."

"Billy, there's nothing wrong with Sheriff Logan. He's a good man in my book."

"The stinkin' sidewinder put you into that infernal prison. I don't reckon we need help from his kind. He'd probably find a way to get me and Thorn here into that dratted cage he's got."

"Calm down, Billy. You can't blame Sheriff Logan for putting me in prison. It was his job to uphold the law. It was Wes who put me in prison with his lying."

"The man coulda believed what you said when you told him you didn't do the shooting. He knew as well as anybody else in town did that Wes Lane was a no-good liar. So did that put-on fake of a judge what sentenced you to five years in that horrible place. I'm plumb convinced the judge was looking after the son of his old friend Major Lane. I ain't got no use for either one of them."

"It's over now, Billy. Forget it. Resentment against those men won't get me my time back, and it sure won't help me recover my horses. I'll stay here overnight, and you can show me around tomorrow. I'll ride Pitch back to town tomorrow and take the steel dust back to Burt Glassner at the livery. While I'm in town, I'll talk to Logan about the stolen horses."

"Good luck riding that black devil horse. You sure named him right. I tried to ride him once, and he pitched me off on his first jump. I thought he'd broken me in two, and that's a fact. There was a time I was named a top bronc buster, but he's more than I want to try."

"You could ride him, Billy. He just likes to show off. Pitch quit trying to throw me when he found out I was determined to ride him."

"Huh. He just likes you for some unknown reason and hates everybody else in the world."

Billy pushed back his chair and got up to walk to the corner bunks. Taking up a quilt and folding it, he turned to hang it on the ladder leading to the loft. "I'm going out to put that horse into a stall for you, Red, then I'm sleeping upstairs. You take my bunk, so's you and your dad can talk some tonight. I'll see you two in the morning."

Billy turned to go outside, then turned back. "We've got to have us a talk before you leave for town in the morning. Thorn and me made some different arrangements about the cattle you don't know about yet. He'll tell you about it." Billy went outside.

"Exactly what did Billy mean about making different arrangements about the cattle, Dad?"

"We lost a lot of cattle that first winter, son. We made a trip up there every few weeks when the weather let us, and we cleared out most of the wolves that were ragging on them. Billy even got him a good-sized bear right out here in our pasture."

Will shook his head. "A good third of the stock didn't make it through, even with all the hay you and the hands stacked. That was a really bad winter, and we were horrified when we got up there and found we had lost so many cows. We knew something had to be done.

"Billy went over to Benton to see some of his people. He found a fella who had good pasture on the other side of the mountains, bordering the reservation lands. He generally raises horses, not cattle, but he agreed to winter the herd in exchange for every fourth calf. I signed an agreement with him, and that's what we've done the last two years.

"I hated to lose the calves, with the herd numbers down like they were, but I believed we'd lose many more by leaving the herd up high another winter. Another thing—there was no way Billy and I could hire help to cut half the amount of hay you managed to get up there the first winter, and it turned out that wasn't anywhere near enough."

"You did right, Dad. I would have done the same thing."

"I'm glad to hear you say that, son. I know you set some store by those red cattle, and I worried, but Billy and I did the best we knew how.

"It's almost time to move the cows up to the high pastures. We had to pay ten head of grown stuff to get enough riders to help us last year. I reckon we'll have to do the same again."

"No, you won't. I've got a little money. Remember I wrote you that the man I was working for let us work an extra day a week for wages?"

"Sure, I remember."

"Well, I worked every Saturday, and I've got enough to hire a couple of riders for a week or two to get the branding done and move the herd."

"That's a blessing, Red. It'll sure make Billy happy. He hated giving up those cows. It'll be good to tell him."

"I've got to make a trip to town to take that horse back, so I'll pick up some supplies. Do you have some idea where we could get a couple of riders?"

"I think we can get those two boys that helped us last year and the year before. They'll come cheap too. They'll be tickled to get their hands on some cash money."

Red and his father sipped innumerable cups of coffee and talked until after midnight. One or the other occasionally got out of his chair to add a log to the fire.

When they finally both ran out of words, Red banked

the fire with a piece of green oak and crawled into the top bunk. He was asleep when his head hit the pillow.

The bright sun shone in the side window when he woke up. Most of the snow on the road had melted during the night. Red ate the breakfast Billy insisted on cooking, then stood up to shrug into his coat.

"I'm going to have to deal with that fool horse for a while," he said. "I'll get Pitch settled down as quickly as I can. Then we'll ride over to White Willow Ranch and look around before we go to town."

"You won't see much in the daylight," Will said, "That Gilbert Patten keeps a bunch of guards around, and they don't let nobody onto the place."

"Burt Glassner told me Major Lane was killed and Gil Patten took over White Willow. Do you think Wes could still be there?" Red asked.

"If he is, he's in the graveyard along with his kinfolk," Will replied. "That boy would never stay holed up at the ranch for months at the time. He'da been in town carousing at the Red Wheel or causing somebody some trouble.

He looked sharply at Red. "Do you think you'll ever be able to prove it was Wes that actually shot Johnny Yates, Red?"

Will pulled a heavy sweater over his head. "I know there's been talk in town. A lot of the men got to wondering about things after you went away. They knew full well you'd never been known to drink much, and Wes drank frequently. They also knew Wes was a liar.

And that Jack Dolman sure acted awful funny after the trial. He came out here and told me you weren't drunk that night, like he testified for you at the trial, but ever since then he's acted like he doesn't even know me. Whenever I see him on the street in town, he turns and goes some other way."

"You know something, Dad? Burt told me he saw Major Lane and Jack Dolman go into Ben Seymour's office together the day before the major was killed. Do you think that visit could have had anything to do with me and that shooting?"

"I've thought from the beginning that the major mighta made some kind of deal with the judge to get you such a light sentence, Red. If what Wes said at your trial would have been true, you woulda hanged. Lane knew exactly what he had in Wes, but he loved the boy, and we both know he would have protected him any way he could."

"I know where Wes probably is." Billy pulled on his coat.

Will and Red turned to stare at him.

"Major Lane had him a big place down near Guadala-jara somewhere. I've heard Wes talking about it. He's probably hiding out down there, waiting until some-body cleans Patten's crooks out of White Willow. It's either that or his pa mighta made him agree to stay down there so's he'd be safe."

"Well, we're not going to solve anything by talking." Red crossed the cabin to open the door. He called over his shoulder as he stepped outside. "Let's go check on those horses."

Red whistled as he stepped through the gate into the pasture. Pitch's head jerked high. He turned to stare up the hill. Red whistled again. Hooves pounding, Pitch ran toward the sound, the mares and foals running in his wake.

Standing still, Red held his hat down at his side and whistled again as the black slid to a stop about twenty feet in front of him. Snorting and tossing his head, the horse circled and reared, circled and reared, staying inches out of Red's reach.

Softly coaxing, Red walked toward Pitch. "Come on, boy. I've got some sugar in my pocket. Come on. We've got some riding to do."

Ears flat, Pitch stood still, visibly trembling. Red held out a lump of sugar. The horse watched him a moment, then, lifting his hooves daintily, stepped forward to drop his soft nose into Red's hand to take the treat.

Murmuring soft words, Red slid his left hand along the horse's nose, then up between his eyes to scratch between his ears. Pitch stepped closer and pushed his head against Red's middle.

"Are you glad to see me, old boy? Let's get you saddled and see if you'll still let me ride."

Pitch seemed eager for the bridle and stood still for Red to settle the pad and saddle and pull the cinch strap tight. The horse sunfished a little when he felt Red's weight in the stirrup, but as soon as Red settled into the saddle, Pitch behaved as well as if he was ridden every day.

"Well, I'da never believed it if I hadn't seen it with my own eyes. That wild varmint earned his name by pitching every other rider that ever tried to sit him into the dirt. I guess he's what you'd call a one-man horse."

"I don't know about that, Billy. Becky McClain used to ride him."

Billy turned away and stomped into the dimness of the big barn, cursing under his breath.

Red chuckled to himself.

Becky really did ride Pitch once, but she was sitting in the saddle in front of me when she did it.

Chapter Nine

When Billy and Red approached a curve in the road a short distance from the entrance to White Willow Ranch, Red moved off into the brush and dismounted. Motioning for Billy to follow, he led Pitch to a spot where he couldn't be seen from the road.

Leaning close to Billy, he whispered, "Stay with me. I want to get as close as we can and see if we can find out what's going on."

Walking on the balls of his feet and watching where he stepped, Red walked as quietly as he could. He knew Billy was close behind him, moving silently. Waving a hand for Billy to stop, he crouched behind a clump of box elders.

Red carefully parted the branches to look toward the gate. He almost swore aloud when he saw five of his young horses grazing peacefully in the field in front of the ranch house. Two men sat their horses about ten feet beyond the gate.

Billy almost growled when he saw them. "What did I tell you? Them fellas is some of those hard cases what ride with Patten. I think I recognize the little one on the light-colored horse. He looks a whole lot like Cole Wilson, the Red River gunfighter. I had him pointed out to me oncet down to Gila Bend."

"Well, I'm going to go over there and tell them I saw my horses in that field, and I came to fetch them home."

"You're plumb crazy, boy. You'll be lucky if you don't get a bullet for your trouble."

"I've got a gun too, old man. I'm not so sure they'll be hard to get along with as long as we both ride over there with our saddle guns across our laps." Red turned away from the bushes. "Let's go back and get our horses."

They both mounted, leaving the steel dust tied. They leaned forward to remove their rifles from their saddles and held them across their laps with their fingers on the triggers. At Red's signal, he and Billy walked their horses into the road and around the curve to approach the gate.

The small man on the light-colored horse moved closer to the fence, his left hand lying on his pistol grip. He asked, "What do you men want here?"

Red lifted the business end of his rifle slightly so the man noticed it. The fellow instantly moved his hand away from his pistol.

"I've some business with the man in charge of the ranch."

"I'm in charge here. You can tell me your business."

"Mister, I want to talk to whoever is running White Willow Ranch."

"I told you, fella. Whatever you have to say, you can say it to me."

"All right, I'll just do that. You and your sidekick here just run on up to the house and tell your boss that Red Thornton was here and sent him this message. I want my horses. That's all. I want my horses back, and I want them back within twenty-four hours, or I'm coming to take them back."

The rider on the spotted horse nosed his animal close to the light-colored horse. His voice had a sneer in it. "You're a dead man if you try it, Thornton. Those horses belong to White Willow Ranch now. We're going to slap a brand on them as soon as the weather warms up enough so we can work outside."

"Tell your boss to catch one of those yearlings and look up under his mane. He'll want to return them to where he found them, and he'll thank me for saving him from hanging as a horse thief. If Sheriff Logan wires the United States Marshal's office that we've got a gang of horse thieves up here, they'll send somebody pronto."

"What the dickens are you blathering about?"

"I think I spoke pretty plain, fella. My stock is marked the day it's foaled, and the marks are registered at the courthouse. You just run on down to the house and tell your boss to take himself a look. Tell him I said to be careful getting them back up the mountain. I don't want any of them damaged."

Backing Pitch away from the gate, Red kept his rifle aimed in the direction of the two men until he was out of pistol range. Turning his horse but holding him to a walk, he left, Billy riding beside him.

Before they rode into the trees lining the road, Red heard the sound of a galloping horse. One of the guards stayed at the gate, and the other fanned his horse toward the ranch house.

"Let's go to town, Billy. I'll get you to return this steel dust to Burt at the livery while I go talk to Sheriff Logan. Thank Burt for the loan of the horse for me, please."

"I'll do that. I'm looking forward to a cool beer."

"That sounds good, but I figure I should go have a long talk with that lawyer. I've got a feeling I'd better know a little bit more about what's been going on around here."

"Wait a minute. Please explain what the heck good it is telling Patten your horses are branded and registered. Crooks don't care about nothing like that."

"Believe me, Billy, Patten will care. He's hiding out in that ranch for some reason that's important to him. I don't know what it is, but it's big. He doesn't want anything to do with any U.S. Marshal.

"I'll bet you money my stock will be back in your pasture when we get home. If they're not, he'll have to find another hideout, and he knows it. I don't think a few yearlings will be worth it for him to risk his safety."

Sheriff Logan wasn't in his office, so Red decided to go on across the street to Ben Seymour's law office. He wanted to thank him for trying to help him at his trial and see if he had been paid. He didn't know if Seymour would tell him anything, but he might be able to find out whether Wes was still alive.

Seymour's office was the whole second floor of the building that housed the town's barbershop. Just about the time Red reached the outside stairs and started to climb up, Dale and Willie Milton stepped out of the barbershop door. They almost walked into him.

The brothers were never really close friends of Red's, but they were certainly speaking acquaintances. Their ranch was less than ten miles from Heard's Mountain, and they'd gone to the same school he did.

When the Miltons recognized Red, they lowered their eyes to look at the sidewalk, turned their faces away, and walked around him.

It was all Red could do to keep from yelling at the two men—saying what fools they were. His cheeks burned with a surge of anger that left him trembling and gritting his teeth.

Those two boys are a long way from being angels themselves. Maybe folks will find out the truth someday. I guess I'll just have to wait it out.

Holding on to the rail with his left hand, he climbed

the creaky wooden stairs to the door of Seymour's office. When he reached the top, he turned to see the Milton brothers standing on the far side of the street, looking up at him.

Ignoring their stares, he opened the door marked BENJAMIN SEYMOUR, ATTORNEY-AT-LAW, and stepped into a small reception room. A stiff-looking young man in a brown suit sat behind a polished table with an open ledger in front of him.

He looked at Red over his glasses, an annoyed expression on his face. "May I help you, sir?"

Not liking the man's tone of voice, Red answered in kind. "I'm Rufus Thornton, and I'm here to see Ben Seymour."

The man's expression and the sound of his voice changed instantly from cold annoyance to warm welcoming. He stood up and leaned slightly forward.

It was astonishing.

"I am so sorry, Mr. Thornton. Mr. Seymour is out of town. I don't expect him back for at least a week. He'll be terribly distressed that he missed you. I expect him back on the ninth. Could I make an appointment, or would you prefer he come out to your ranch? He would hate to cause you to make an extra trip to town."

It took Red a moment or two to process the man's words.

What in the world is wrong with this fella? I've never seen such an about-face in my life. He's almost babbling.

Why should he or Seymour care about missing me or making me come back into town?

"I'll come back in a couple of weeks. Don't bother to make an appointment. I can't be sure of the exact day."

"That's perfectly all right, Mr. Thornton. Mr. Seymour will make time for you whenever you can make it back to town."

The man still stood behind his table as Red left the room.

He walked down the steps to the street, shaking his head as he tried to puzzle out why his presence would make Seymour's secretary act so crazy.

He stopped for a moment and muttered to himself, "You'da thought I was Major Lane himself, come back to life."

I'll order the supplies we'll need and go get some food over at McClain's place. There's no need of me wondering over what's wrong with that secretary. I'll find out when I come back to town.

McClain's café was crowded. Red waited a few minutes for one of the tables to empty before he could sit down to order his dinner. He watched Jeannie as she walked briskly among the tables, smiling and speaking first to one customer and then another. Her words and expression were friendly but businesslike.

A boy who looked to be about ten or twelve was clearing tables. Red kept his eyes on Jeannie and avoided the stares of the other diners. As soon as Red took a seat, Jeannie brought him a handwritten menu.

"Good morning, Red. It's good to see you. Dad made his 'poor man's dinner' today. It's a tender roast with lots of vegetables. Everyone says it's delicious. Will that be all right? I made bread to go with it."

"Anything you have, Jeannie. I'm always hungry, and a roast sounds great. I'd like some coffee with it."

"Of course, and a piece of pie—it's apple. I'll be right back."

She turned to weave her way among tables back to the kitchen. Red kept his eyes down, ignoring the buzz of talk that broke out throughout the room when she closed the door behind her.

The crowd thinned out by the time Red finished his meal. Jeannie suddenly stood at his elbow with a steaming coffeepot and a big slice of apple pie.

Red smiled up at her and said, "Take a breather, Jeannie. Sit down and talk to me. You'll run yourself to death, the way you're going. I've been watching you work. You haven't slowed down even once since I walked in the door."

Jeannie laughed and put the pie and coffeepot on the table. "I can take a little rest and drink a cup of coffee now. I'll go get me a cup."

She walked over to get a clean coffee cup from behind the counter and whispered something to her father. He lifted his head to glare at Red. Returning to the table, Jeannie slid into the chair opposite Red.

"I've been in a flutter since before breakfast this morning. This place is getting busier every day. If business keeps on growing like it has lately, I'll have to hire someone to help me serve. Supper business is even busier than this. I hate to have to hire somebody, because it'll cut into our profit, and this is our only income."

"You've been forced to grow up fast, Jeannie, with this café to run and Becky's baby to raise."

"I wanted to take care of Becky's baby, Red. I couldn't part with Joey. He's all I have left of my sister. A lot of people tried to make me give him up, my father included, but I never will. I don't care how much they nag at me.

"That Reverend Sylvester has been the worst of all. He just won't leave it alone. I can't really avoid him, keeping a public place like this. He keeps threatening to go to law to get Joey away from me, but Sheriff Logan says to ignore him."

Jeannie's checks flushed with pink, and her eyes seemed to flash as she leaned forward to whisper, "That sorry Gilbert Patten even tried to frighten me about Joey the other day."

"What do you mean, he tried to frighten you?"

"Patten and two of those men of his came in here the other day and insisted on seeing Joey. I told them to get out, and they got loud about it.

"He kept on reminding me that Joey was Wes Lane's boy as well as Becky's. He said it over and over. He went on talking, saying he was the only friend Wes had left in Acorn Creek, and he was always there to take his side. He kept smiling down at me and saying Wes needed to see his boy, and he would see him soon.

"When I asked him what that meant, he said Wes would be home soon, that he was probably on his way right now. I don't know if he was lying to scare me, or what.

"To be honest, though, I *was* scared half to death, but Sheriff Logan walked in the door about that time. When Patten and his two friends saw him come in, they didn't say another word. They just got up and left.

"I worry they'll come back, though. I haven't let Joey come into the café since the day it happened."

"What do you think they'll do, Jeannie? Surely they wouldn't try to hurt a little kid. Heck, the whole countryside would be down on them if they tried a fool trick like that."

"I don't know what they mean to do, Red. It scares me to try to think what might be in Patten's mind. It scares me silly to think of Wes coming back and trying to take Joey away from me too.

"Sometimes I think I'll have to take him and go somewhere where nobody knows us to keep him safe."

"You won't have to do that, Jeannie. Sheriff Logan thinks Patten or one of his men probably killed Wes. If he is alive and just hiding out somewhere, he's probably afraid to come back here."

"I don't think so, Red. Wes is a little crazy—you know he is. He's crazy enough to eventually come back to Acorn Creek. I'm sure of that. It doesn't matter to him if people come to think he lied about you. He doesn't care."

"Do you really think Patten knew what he was talking about?" Red asked.

"There was a certain tone to Patten's voice when he said Wes was coming home soon. I believed him. It was obvious he knows more than he was saying. If Wes does come home and tries to take Joey, I'm going someplace where he can't find us."

Red's voice almost broke as he leaned across the table to whisper, "Jeannie, please don't leave Acorn Creek without letting me know how to find you."

Jeannie's eyes widened, and her lips softened into a smile. "I'll let you know, Red. I promise I will."

Still smiling, Jeannie stood up, picking up her cup in one hand and the coffeepot in the other. "Finish your pie, now. I have work to do."

Red watched as she walked away from him.

Jeannie's grown up. She might not be much more than seventeen, but she's a beautiful woman. It got downright hard for me to breathe, watching her eyes flash with anger when she talked about Patten and his men.

I wish I'd been here when they came in. I'd like to scare those low-down suckers a little. I'd like to scare them with a double-barrel shotgun.

Burning with anger that Patten and his men would frighten Jeannie, Red lowered his flushed face and finished his coffee, silently telling himself to calm down.

Returning to the mercantile, Red picked up the two cloth sacks of supplies the storekeeper had prepared for him. Billy was waiting, sitting his horse when Red came out of the store. Tying the sacks behind Pitch's saddle, Red climbed on and headed for home.

He hardly remembered the trip back to Heard's Mountain. Most of the way was spent going over and over his anger at the nerve of Gil Patten.

Red told himself his anger was because the man had dared to take his yearlings. But his memory of the stark terror on Jeannie McClain's face when she confessed her fear that Patten would harm little Joey mingled in with every thought. On top of that, she had to worry that Wes would come back and try to take the boy away from her.

On the ride to Chief Billy's cabin, Red repeated to himself each word he'd exchanged with Jeannie. He could see every feature of her face, the curve of her lips, the blue flash of her eyes.

He was thinking so hard, it surprised him when Pitch came to a halt with his head and shoulders already inside the wide barn door. Billy had dismounted and was tending his horse, his back to Red.

Red spoke to Pitch and rode him straight into the barn. Dismounting, he unsaddled, led the horse into a stall, and then spent a few minutes rubbing him down while the horse ate a small bait of oats. When he finished, he picked up the last bag of supplies and started for the house.

When he walked out of the barn door facing the cabin, the first thing he saw was the group of yearlings contentedly grazing beyond the corral fence. He stopped and stared.

How the devil did I miss seeing those horses when I came in a while ago? I musta been lost in thought.

Chapter Ten

Billy and Red rode single file along a track crossing the river on the White Willow range, several miles below the main house. They'd left Billy's cabin in the gray light of dawn and circled around the edge of the mountains where the Thornton herd grazed in the high meadows from spring to early fall.

The cattle had wintered on property bordering Billy's sister's homestead for the past two years. Billy planned for him and Red to eat breakfast with his youngest sister and ask her two teenage boys to ride with them to help brand the cattle and move them into the hills for the summer.

"Those two boys will be over the moon to get their hands on some cash money, Red. It won't take much.

We had to give 'em ten cows last year, but their mother wouldn't let 'em be sold.

"Willie Mae knew if the boys sold the critters, she'd probably never see a cent of the money, so she made the deal with me. The boys didn't like it one bit, but there wasn't much they could say. She was going to pay the fella who owned the property herself and then share the beef with some of our other kin and a couple of her neighbors.

"We'll still have to give her a couple of cows this year, Red. She's the one her neighbors depend on to help when they hit hard times. Ned and Little Yellow Bird will work better, though, when they know they'll end up with a little bit of cash in their pockets."

"How long do you think it will it take to get the herd up to the pasture?"

"No more than a day, but it'll take us three or four days if not longer to do the branding and get them ready to go."

"I just wondered. I've got some things I want to do as soon as I can get back to town."

Billy nudged his horse with his heels and led the way. The sun was high when they came out of the woods into a small field. A low-roofed cabin nestled among a large group of ancient ponderosa pines.

Billy dismounted to slide the gate poles to one side so they could turn their horses into the empty corral.

"Why don't they have any horses in the corral, Billy?"

"Most of their horses are like pets. All they have to do is whistle, and they come running. So they just turn 'em loose most of the time."

"I could probably do that with Pitch, but I'd never be sure. He might take a notion one day to take his family and head for the mountains on his own."

"I wouldn't give him the chance. He's ornery enough to take off with every horse we've got."

Smiling at the venom that filled Billy's voice whenever he talked about the black mustang, Red followed him to the back door of the house.

Billy shook the plank door and yelled, "Hello the house! Where the heck is everybody?"

Willie Mae yelled back as she came to unlatch the door, "We were in our beds, sleeping as sensible people do, before we heard you clattering into our yard, making noise like a white man."

Billy reached past the door to grab his sister in a bear hug and laughed aloud as he said, "What do you mean, 'like a white man'? I can still out-Indian anybody on this reservation."

"Don't you ever forget, big brother, you're not on the reservation here. This land is mine from my husband, and it will belong to my sons. This has never been reservation land."

The tiny woman's voice was soft, but each word seemed to have a sharp edge. Though her head only came up to the middle of Billy's chest, she had no trouble challenging her brother.

He stepped aside and waved one hand toward Red, saying. "There's your clumsy white man. He's the one making all the noise."

"I am so glad to see you, Red. The tinker stopped in yesterday and told us you were back home at last. I am happy to see you are well." Willie Mae smiled broadly and held out both hands.

Red took her hands in his and smiled down into her welcoming face. "Thank you, little sister. I'm sure glad to be home. I'm looking forward to one of your fine breakfasts. Did your brother think to send you word we were coming this morning?"

"My brother never thinks of things like that, Red, but you are always welcome at my table—both of you. Come on in. The coffee's almost ready. My boys are up, and breakfast will be only a few minutes."

Dressed in tight jeans and a plaid shirt that looked as if they were made for a young boy, Willie Mae rushed around preparing the meal. She deftly filled two large iron skillets with thick slices of bacon and set them on the top of the cookstove. Washing her hands, she measured flour into a large bowl, then added salt, soda, and buttermilk. She dug into the mass with both hands to mix it.

Once the biscuits were rolled out and shaped, she slid the pan into the oven. Twice she turned the strips of bacon and then began to break eggs into a deep bowl for scrambling. In minutes, eggs done to a turn, crisp bacon, and three dozen large, perfectly browned biscuits were on the table.

Just as Willie Mae put the breakfast onto the table, her two sons joined Billy and Red, taking seats on a bench behind the table. Hardly speaking throughout the meal, the four men and Willie Mae ate all of the food, adding scoops of sweet butter and tablespoons of wild honey.

"Oh, my goodness, that was good," Red said, holding his cup out for Willie Mae to refill it with strong black coffee.

"You can say that again. I don't know how my two nephews keep from getting as round as they are tall," Billy remarked.

"You ate as much as we did, Uncle," the boys said in unison.

"Yeah, but I'm a sight bigger than either one of you. I reckon I *should* eat more than you do."

"Not so," the tallest of the boys said. "Ma says we eat a lot because we're growing fast. Old people like you stopped growing long ago. *You'll* get fat if you keep on eating like that."

"I see you're not only growing taller, Ned Barker, but sassier. Do you think you should speak to your uncle so?" Billy growled.

The boy turned his head to one side and stared at Billy out of the corner of his eyes. He hesitated, evidently trying to determine if his uncle was serious. "I beg your pardon, Uncle. I did not mean to offend you."

"You didn't offend me, son. I was just teasing. You're right about me eating a lot. Your mother's cooking tastes like home to me." Billy chuckled.

Smiling, the smaller boy—the one Billy called Little Yellow Bird—punched his brother's shoulder and said, "Come, Ned, let's get our horses saddled."

"I want to tell you something before you go to get your horses saddled, nephew. This year Mr. Thornton has cash money to pay you for your work. He offers to give your mother two cows to pay her for the use of her wagon and tools. He will pay each of you ten dollars for helping us brand the cattle and drive them to the high meadows."

Eyes shining, both boys nodded their agreement without speaking and turned to run outside, slamming the door. Red looked over at Billy and smiled when they heard the boys whooping and yelling in delight as they crossed the yard.

The branding went smoothly, taking an entire week, two days longer than Billy had estimated. The calf crop was larger than Red had hoped, and even with paying one in four calves for the use of winter pasture, the herd had grown more than he'd anticipated, totaling more than three hundred head. He couldn't stop smiling his delight at the number of cattle and their fine condition.

By the end of the week, Red's legs and back ached. He had worked hard at Yuma, but this work used completely different muscles. He fought to keep his discomfort out of his face, slowly straightening his back as he stood up from branding, hoping it was the last calf.

"How are we doing, Billy?" he called.

Billy walked his horse closer to the fire and took off

his hat to fan his face as he said, "That's it, Red. That's every last one of the blasted little horned devils. I'm ready for a bath, one of little sister's good suppers, and one night in a real bed before we start pushing these ornery critters up that mountain."

He dismounted and joined Red beside the fire. "Those two boys are down at the creek, washing off some of the stink. That ice water don't bother them youngsters none at all. I'm about as nasty as I've ever been in my life, but I don't think I can face washing in cold water."

"You nor me either, Billy. I'm downright filthy myself, even if I haven't been cutting the calves like you were. Let's get everything together and the wagon packed so we can leave as soon as the boys get back here."

"We're mostly ready. Everybody's bedrolls are already in the wagon. Put that hot branding iron in a bucket of sand before you put it into the wagon so it won't set something alight. I'll catch up the horses and get 'em harnessed."

Billy turned away. "Wait a minute, Red. Who's that riding in? Wait a minute. I'll be darned if it ain't John Wallace Barrone. He's the big honcho over to the reservation. I don't know the others—don't know as I ever saw them before. I wonder what in the Sam Hill they could want?"

"Look, Billy—isn't that a body tied on that roan Barrone's leading?"

"I do believe it is. Lord knows what's up now."

John Wallace Barrone waved to Billy and Red as the three horsemen drew near the fire. He appeared a foot taller than the men who rode beside him. All three carried rifles across the pommel of their saddles.

Barrone wore a flat-crowned black hat pulled down almost to his eyebrows and a leather coat with a thick fur collar. His expression was stern, and his black eyes seemed fierce and angry.

"Get down and join us, Mr. Barrone," Red said, moving to the side of the Indian's horse. "I'll push the pot back onto the hot coals, and we'll have some coffee."

"I did not come here for your coffee, Thornton. I came to bring you this dead man."

"Who is it, and why in the world would you bring a dead man to me?"

"The man's papers say he is a deputy United States Marshal. We found him lying dead in his camp near Glade Spring early this morning. He is the third man to be murdered along the old outlaw trail in two months."

"Murdered? Why? What do you mean?"

"A month ago, a man of my people came to my cabin badly wounded. He told me he was shot by a group of men he met on the old outlaw trail. The man did not live. He had bled too much.

"Two weeks ago a man of our village went onto the mountain early one morning to hunt and did not come back. The next day, his sons went to search for him.

They found him lying beside the old outlaw trail with five bullets in his back.

"They brought their father's body home and came to tell me what happened. These two men and I searched along the trail and found many tracks of a group of riders passing. The tracks led east.

"I reported both murders to the agent at the reservation, but he did not even go to the mountains to look. He says they were only hunting accidents, not murders. He will do nothing.

"These two men and I rode to the mountain to hunt deer this morning. We reached there before light. We planned to stop at Glade Spring at sunrise and make coffee to warm us.

"When we got to the spring, we found this man. He was murdered exactly as our young man was. He lay in his blankets with bullets in his back. I counted five.

"He was given no chance to defend himself but was murdered as he slept. We found many tracks of shod horses around his campsite. They rode east toward your father's ranch."

"The outlaw trail doesn't lead to our ranch, sir." Red's voice hardened. His face flushed in anger, and he stepped closer to John Wallace Barrone's horse. "As you know very well, the trail dips close to our land but makes a turn about halfway down the mountain and goes directly to White Willow Ranch."

John Wallace Barrone looked down at Red's angry face and hesitated a moment before he said, "The man's papers say this is a United States Marshal, and he is a white man. He must be turned over to a sheriff.

"I know that if I take this body into Acorn Creek, Sheriff Logan or some of the people of the town will say I killed him."

"You may be right, at that. I'll take him to Sheriff Logan."

"The roan is the man's own horse. We found it hobbled near his camp." Holding out his hand to Red, he said, "I put everything, including his guns, back into his saddlebags. Everything except this badge."

Still angry, Red watched John Wallace Barrone's face as he reached up to hold his hand out for the badge.

Without another word, Barrone dropped the badge into his hand and turned to ride back the way he'd come, dropping the reins of the roan so it would stand ground hitched. The two other men followed.

"Well, I'll be a something or other." Billy squatted down near the fire and pushed his hat up to scratch his head. "What do you think of that?"

"I don't know what to think, Billy. There for a minute I thought he was trying to accuse me of something."

"Barrone knows where that trail goes. He just wanted to take a jab at you. He's got no use for your father, you know."

"No, I did not know. Why does he have no use for my father?"

"It's something Thorn is going to have to explain to

you his own self, boy. It ain't my place, and I ain't gonna do it."

"Well, the devil with you too," Red muttered.

Grabbing up the reins of the roan, Red tied the two strips of leather together and led the horse closer to his. Untying his rope, he slid it through the loop. Once the horse was secured, he turned back to the fire to help load the wagon.

Billy stood up and straightened his hat as he said, "You ain't got no cause to get mad at me just because you and Thorn don't talk like you should."

"Oh, shut up, and let's get ready to go."

Neither man spoke on the way back to the barn. When Billy turned the wagon into the yard, Ned and Little Yellow Bird sat on the top rail of the corral fence waiting for them.

"Come help us get this wagon unloaded, boys!" Billy yelled to his nephews, his voice raspy. "This ain't no picnic we're having. We've got to get everything ready to leave out of here before light in the morning."

Ned jumped down from the corral fence and, followed by his younger brother, ran to their uncle. When Billy's feet hit the ground, he turned to find his nephews standing close by, looking up at him.

"My mother says we can't go up onto the mountain tomorrow—that some men are killing people up there," Ned whispered.

Placing one hand on the shoulder of each boy, Billy

said, "Don't you boys be worrying. I'll talk to your ma. We're not going to camp near that outlaw trail."

"She says they might be ghosts—even shape-shifters."

"They are not. Ghosts and shape-shifters don't use guns to kill people. Stop your worrying like I said, and help us get this stuff put away. I told you I'd talk to your ma—it'll be all right."

Willie Mae came out of her back door and approached the wagon. "Did John Wallace Barrone find you, my brother?"

"He did, little sister. I am sorry Barrone worried you. I will not put your sons in danger."

"How can you not if you go to the mountains where men are murdered for no reason?"

"We will not camp near the outlaw trail. When we come near it, I will scout ahead and make sure there is no one there before the boys take the cattle across. Red and I know a cave near the top of Cedar Mountain where we have camped many times. We will be safe there. It is far away from the trail."

"I know my sons are almost men, but I am afraid."

"They will be safe. They have their guns, and I have mine. We were warned. The other men were not—they did not expect men to shoot at them. Do not worry. We will be gone only tomorrow and tomorrow night. I will have your boys back here to you before the sun is high on Thursday."

Bowing her head, Willie Mae turned to walk back to the house.

She stopped at the door and called out, "I have water heating. The boys can bring it to you in the tack room. You men must bathe before you come into my house."

Billy laughed. "I think she's a little bit peeved with me."

"I don't blame her much. Getting peeved with you is downright easy."

"Come on, Red. You can't stay in a snit forever."

"Huh."

Red went into the tack room to find an empty galvanized washtub sitting in the middle of the floor. Ned brought in buckets of cold water from the well, and Little Yellow Bird poured in two buckets of steaming water heated to boiling on Willie Mae's cookstove.

Stripping off his clothes, Red slid into the tub and scrubbed off the dust and sweat accumulated over a week of working from dawn to dusk.

Finally clean, he dressed in spare jeans and shirt and went out to take a seat on the top rail of the corral fence beside Ned and Little Yellow Bird to wait for Billy to get the tub emptied and refilled so he could bathe.

"I thought you were going to take all night. We're about to starve," he chided Billy when the chief returned.

"I didn't take as long as you did, Red Thornton. Come on to the house if you're so all-fired hungry."

After eating supper, Red pulled on his jacket and gloves and wrapped a wool scarf around his neck. "I'll take the man's body on down to Acorn Creek, Billy. It'll be near midnight when I get there, but I don't want to wait on this. Pitch knows the trail well enough to follow it until the moon comes up.

"Sheriff Logan needs to telegraph the marshal's office and get somebody up here pronto. I expect this will do the trick to get rid of Gil Patten and his cronies."

"You sure that's who all is doing the shooting?"

"I'm not sure, but I'm certainly thinking that way. It could be some of Patten's men who don't follow orders too well. Patten probably doesn't even know about the killings yet. I can't imagine he would want to do anything to call attention to his escape route. White Willow makes a perfect hideout if nobody knows about them using the old trail.

"You take care with those boys, Billy. Don't let anything happen to them. Make camp in the cave at the top. I'll meet you there if I don't join you earlier. I'll come up the back trail from our ranch. That's the shortest way."

"You take care too, son. We'll see you sometime tomorrow."

Leading the roan, Red followed the route he and Billy had taken the day before until he came to the cutoff leading over to the main road to Acorn Creek. When he reached the town, neither Sheriff Logan nor Leon was at the office. The only light burning on the street shone out of the open doorway of the hotel.

He tied his horse and the roan in front of the building and started up the steps.

"Who's on the horse, Red?" Sheriff Logan asked as he emerged from the shadows on the porch.

"It's a United States Marshal, Sheriff. John Wallace Barrone and two of his men found him up at Glade Spring alongside the old outlaw trail. He's packing five slugs in his back. Barrone said he was shot while he lay in his blankets."

"Lord have mercy. I'll have to telegraph the marshal's headquarters and let them know. Did you find out the man's name?"

"I haven't been through his belongings. I figured it was your job to do that. Barrone said he packed all his things back into his saddlebags. Here's his badge. Barrone brought the body to me where we were branding our new calves. He said he feared he would be blamed for the killing if he brought the body in."

"I might not jump to blame him for it, but I'm afraid there's some people around here that would."

"I'm gonna take my horse over to the livery, and I'm not staying up long. I need to catch me a few hours sleep so I can get on back up on the mountain before tomorrow night. Billy and two of his nephews are pushing my herd up to the summer pasture."

"Wait 'til I walk down past the church and get Jed Martindale up so he can take care of the body."

"That horse is tied, and the man sure ain't going anywhere. I've told you all I know. You can figure out anything else you need yourself."

"Well, go ahead, then, if you feel that way about it. I'll take care of everything."

Pushing his horse, Red reached the top pasture by late afternoon. He loosened the cinch on Pitch's saddle and took the bit out of the animal's mouth so it could graze.

Building a fire at the entrance of the cave, he filled his coffeepot and set it on the coals. Leaning back against a rock wall, he rested as the shadows lengthened.

Rearranging the horse's bridle and tightening the saddle cinch, he mounted and walked the horse to a nearby ridge to look over the meadows. He could see cattle moving along slowly. After a few minutes he could hear the high-pitched cries of the two boys and an occasional pop of Billy's whip.

As the herd moved out of the trees and spilled over into the broad meadow, the two boys and Billy worked their way around them and rode straight toward the ridge.

"Do I smell coffee?" Billy yelled as he rode closer.

"I made coffee. Come on up. There's plenty of grass up here for your horses."

When Billy and the two boys came to the campfire, each carried a sack. Billy's held a pot with a bail and an iron rod to make a rack to hang it over the fire. The boys' bags held a fair-sized chunk of venison and some potatoes and onions.

"As you can see, I'm making us some stew. These two are almost impossible to fill up, so I figured it would be the best thing. I'll cut the meat and vegetables small so's they'll hurry up and cook.

"Willie Mae packed us two whole loaves of her white bread, fresh made last night. Soon's I get me a cup of that coffee, I'll get our supper started."

"Did you have any trouble, Billy?"

"We didn't have a minute's trouble Red, and we didn't see a soul. I scouted the trail while the boys pushed the cows up the mountain. The only tracks I found were at least a couple of days old. I went along to the spring. The tracks around there led off down toward White Willow, just like you said."

"I'll bet it was Patten or some of his men. It could be they've been riding out now and then to hold up stages. They probably do their robbing and murdering and then take the old trail back."

"You might be right about that, Red, but they must have another hideout somewhere else. It's a good hundred miles down through the Chocolates to where those coaches are being held up."

"Well, that marshal's being up here looks like somebody's on to them. The man wasn't up here for nothing."

"Pour me some more of that coffee of yours, Red. Though I vow it'll take the lining out of my stomach."

Chapter Eleven

Red left the cave at dawn. He wanted to make sure no one was in the area while Billy boiled a pot of coffee and fried some bacon for their breakfast. Saddling his horse, he rode downhill to Glade Spring.

Finding nothing new there, he turned east along the trail for a short distance but could find no evidence of anyone's passing in the last few hours. When he returned to the cave, he removed his gloves, took the coffee cup Billy handed him, and squatted beside the fire to sip the fiery contents.

"Let's eat up and get moving, fellas. I can't see where anybody's been around to make any tracks since those killers left their tracks around the spring. We'll ride straight down to your sister's house, Billy, and then on back to your cabin the same way we came over."

"Seems reasonable to me."

The ride home by way of Willie Mae's house took most of the day, and Red and Billy reached Heard's Mountain exhausted. Taking time to give the horses a quick rubdown, they walked to the cabin and almost went to sleep eating the supper Will had prepared for them.

"Tell me about the herd, Billy."

"We done good, Thorn. Even paying out a fourth of the calves for two years, we've got us a fine herd. We need to cut out some of the older stock and make a drive over to the railroad. I figure we should sell forty or fifty head."

"That's more than I figured on."

"There's no need feeding those big steers. They'll bring us enough cash to hire a couple of hands and get the ranch going again now that Red's home."

"If that's what Red wants."

Will looked over at his son, an apprehensive expression on his face. Red had studiedly avoided his father's eyes since he came into the cabin.

"What do you say, son?"

Raising his eyes to look his father full in the face, Red said, "I agree with Billy about selling the older stock, but it's up to you to decide."

"No, it's up to all of us. You and Billy have as much work and money in this herd as I do."

"It's all decided, then. Billy wants to sell, I want to sell, and you agree. What are we talking about?"

"What's the matter with you, Red? You're obviously angry about something. I'd like to know what it is."

"I need some sleep right now, Dad. I plan to leave early in the morning. I've got some business to tend to in town. We'll talk later."

Will watched as Red pushed his chair back. He still avoided his father's eyes as he walked over to lie down on his bunk. Without another word, he wrapped his blanket around himself and turned his face to the wall.

Will leaned across the table to whisper, "What the heck's wrong with him, Billy?"

"I ain't in this, Thorn. You need to talk to that boy. He met up with John Wallace Barrone while we were working over there, and Barrone showed him his hate. I told Red to ask you to explain it to him yourself—that it wasn't none of my business."

Without even stopping for coffee, Red left the cabin early and headed to town. He went to the sheriff's office first, but the door was locked, and no one came to the door. Shaking his head in aggravation, he tied his horse in front of Andrew McClain's place and walked down the street to climb the stairs to Attorney Seymour's office.

The same clerk greeted him—still seeming much too happy to see him. "Please have a seat, Mr. Thornton. I'll tell Mr. Seymour you're here."

The man almost jumped to his feet and disappeared down a narrow hallway beyond the desk. Hardly a minute passed before he returned to the room, Ben Seymour walking right behind him.

Smiling, Seymour came around the desk with his hand out. "Thank you for coming all the way into town again to see me, Mr. Thornton. I feared I'd have to come up into the mountains to find you. I'm not very good on horseback these days, and I've heard that road isn't conducive to wheeled traffic. Come on back into my office where we can talk in private."

Red shook the lawyer's extended hand without speaking, busy trying to make some sense of the way both men acted.

The last time I saw Seymour was at my trial, and I definitely got the impression then he was full of impatience with me. He may have even felt a little contempt for me, if I read him right.

There's another thing—he called me Red in those days. I never heard him say Mr. Thornton before today. Why the sudden change? Why the cordial greeting?

I'm not a bit sure what's going on here. I guess if I keep my mouth shut and go along, I'll find out eventually.

"I just dropped in to thank you for the effort you made for me during my trial, Mr. Seymour. I know you didn't have much to work with, so Dad and I truly appreciate your representing me. I'd like to know what your fee is and make arrangements to pay you as soon as I can."

"You don't owe me a thing, son. Forget it. Come on into my private office." Seymour led the way back down the hall and into a large, well-furnished room.

"I have some wonderful news for you. I expect you

probably have some inkling of what it is. Here, take˜ this chair."

As soon as Red was seated, Seymour held out a humidor. "Have a cigar."

Turning to the secretary, who had followed them down the hall and now stood in the office doorway, an expression of avid interest on his face, Seymour said, "Go get Mr. Thornton a cup of coffee, John Asbury."

Red settled himself in the indicated chair and bit the end off the fragrant cigar. Digging into his pocket for a match, he thought, *I guess I'll find out eventually what's come over Seymour. It seems to me the best thing I can do is just keep quiet and watch how this thing comes out.*

Seymour wore a big smile and looked tremendously pleased and satisfied about something as he took the chair behind his big polished desk.

I was certainly never invited to Seymour's office before. He just dropped by the jail a couple of times and acted like he didn't have time to be bothered with me. I'm sure he never believed a word of my story when I told him Wes was lying like a rug and I didn't shoot Johnny Yates.

The secretary came back into the room and handed Red a cup and saucer decorated with flowers and a ring of gold trim around the edge. It held black coffee. With the other hand he held out a small pitcher of cream. Red nodded his thanks for the coffee and waved away the cream.

Seymour motioned for Asbury to leave the room.

The secretary stepped out and closed the door without a sound. Red heard the man's heels click on the wooden floor as he returned to the reception room.

Placing the untouched cup of coffee on the edge of the lawyer's desk, Red leaned forward and asked, "What the devil is going on here, Seymour?"

"I'll explain everything, Mr. Thornton, but first you should read this letter Major Lane left with me to give you."

"Major Lane? Why in the world would Major Lane leave me a letter?"

"Well, you certainly know the man was your uncle. He was your mother's only brother."

"Yes, of course, I knew that, but it never meant much before now."

"Please read your letter, Mr. Thornton. It should explain everything. Major Lane told me it would. I'll have more papers for you when you finish."

Red stared at the familiar writing on the front of the fat envelope. Major Lane had addressed it using his full name, William Rufus Thornton. He'd been called Red so long, his real name looked strange to him.

Shrugging his shoulders, he ripped the envelope open and took out the letter. It felt to be ten pages or more, written in Major Lane's small, precise handwriting.

Dear Red,

*   I want to say* Dear William. *It was my father's name, and your mother's father's as well, of*

course. You certainly know I am your uncle, although our families have been estranged your entire life. I'm sorry we have been apart all these years. There are good reasons for it, and you should know them.

I want to tell you my story, Red. It is your mother's story as well.

I was six years old when Mary Helena was born and our mother died. Somehow I decided my little sister was my child. All our lives I watched over her, cared for her. I crawled out of bed and checked on her in the middle of the night when she was a baby. When she grew big enough to toddle, I made sure she was safe when she played in the yard.

When my little sister was old enough to go to school, I rode with her every morning and waited at the schoolyard gate for her every afternoon. We were inseparable. Seeing her dear little face became as necessary as breathing to me.

Then the War came, and Father pushed me to join the Northern forces. He believed that every man young enough should fight for the Union. I didn't want to leave White Willow, but he was insistent. I finally agreed and went north. I ended up staying away from home almost five long years.

One of the Blairs, an important family in Washington City, was father's dear friend from years before. Father gave me a letter and instructed me to go straight to him when I arrived in the city.

Mr. Blair was able to get me a commission as a lieutenant. I ended up on Grant's staff.

I wanted to leave for home as quickly as I could after Lee surrendered at Appomattox, but because of where I served and an injury I had suffered, many months crawled by before I finally received my discharge.

When I came home and saw Mary Helena again, I could hardly believe my eyes. When I'd left the ranch to go north, she was like a colt. Her hair hung in untidy pigtails, she was all stick-thin arms and legs, and she seemed to grow out of her clothes about once a month. All she seemed interested in then was horses. If she wasn't feeding a new foal or grooming its dam, she was out riding, usually right beside me.

Now, five years later, in place of the colt I met a grown woman. She ran out onto the porch to greet me, and when she threw her arms around me, I noticed her eyes were on a level with mine. It was a terrible shock to me.

She looked so different from the image I'd carried in my heart throughout the War, I could hardly bear to look at her. We spent several days talking about my travels and my adventures. We rode around the ranch together and spent some time getting to know the new horses.

I finally calmed down enough to notice that Mary Helena wasn't saying anything about herself.

Every time we talked, she guided the conversation around to me. I knew from her letters that she continued to go to school after I left to join the military. She even helped to teach the younger children after learning everything the schoolmaster could teach her.

She wasn't the same, though. Before I went away, she told me her every thought, but when I came back, she shut herself away from me. I could tell by her eyes that she was far away in some mysterious women's world I could not fathom. I told myself I could accept the change in her—that it was only Mary Helena growing up—but I found one change I could not accept.

I was at home for about two weeks when Mary Helena came out of her room one Saturday morning in a beautiful white dress with a flowing shawl. She wore a matching hat with a camellia blossom on one side of the brim. Her hair was pinned away from her face, but it hung loose, flowing down her back to almost touch her waist.

She was so beautiful, it hurt. While I stood there staring at her, I heard the sound of wheels on the drive in front of the house. I opened the door and looked out to see your father. He wore a black suit and was driving his buckboard. I remember its wheels were painted red, and somebody had sewn a long, brightly colored cushion for the boards of the front seat.

Will Thornton jumped down from the buckboard and rushed up onto the porch to hold out his right hand to me. He said how glad he was to see I'd made it home all right. I could hardly stand to listen to him.

Just then Mary Helena came out and took Thornton's arm. She kissed me on the cheek and said she would be gone most of the day—that they were going back over to Thornton's place to have a picnic and see his new foals.

I was so shocked, I couldn't even tell them goodbye. If I had tried to speak, I would have cursed Will Thornton. Irrational hate for him surged through me. I wanted to hurt him—I wanted to see him bleed for daring to come near my Mary Helena, much less daring to take her to his house for a picnic, for heaven's sake.

I think I started to realize then that my feelings for my baby sister were much too strong, but I had just lived through that terrible War. I told myself over and over, every day I was away, that I would live to see my family again—that I would come back home and everything would be exactly the same as it was before I left, Father and Mary Helena and me together. A happy family.

I told myself over and over, it was inevitable for a beautiful young woman to meet someone, fall in love, and marry. But I could not bear the thought. Then I told myself it was too soon—she was too young. I convinced myself that Will Thornton could never be good enough for her—not for Mary Helena. As her only brother, I had a responsibility to see that the man she chose was her equal in every way.

Red put the letter down on the edge of the desk. There were more pages, but his eyes kept blurring, and the major's words seemed to be pounding in his brain. He suddenly felt a pressing urge to move around.

Seymour started when he jumped to his feet. Shaking his head at the lawyer, Red stuck his hands into his pockets and walked up and down on the Turkish carpet several times.

Why in the world hasn't Dad told me anything about this—about the major? He should have told me all this himself.

After a few moments he felt calmer and returned to his chair to pick up the last pages of the letter. The major's next words were a shock.

I began to follow Mary Helena every time she left the ranch. If she met Thornton, I joined them. When Thornton came to call on her, I either stayed in the room or stood in the hall and listened to their every word, making sure they knew I was there.

Father fell ill about that time, and Mary Helena stayed at home a lot to take care of him. When he

*died, she came to me the afternoon after his fu-
neral and told me she would marry Thornton immediately. She said he would come for her the
next day.*

*I went a little crazy then. There is no other ex-
planation for what I did.*

*I grabbed Mary Helena by the arm and forced
her upstairs into her bedroom. I slammed the
door and locked it behind her. I then screamed
through the door that she would never marry Will
Thornton.*

*I called him a one-horse rancher and accused
him of being a cow thief. I told her I knew it to be
true, and I would prove it. I swore to her I would
prove he was a thief and see him hang for it.*

*Mary Helena said nothing for a few hours. She
must have been too shocked, too puzzled at my behavior to try to talk to me. Later in the evening she
pounded on the door and cried. She begged me to
let her out, but I refused.*

*As I said earlier, I know now I was a little crazy
then; it is my only excuse for taking such an action.*

*When your father came for her, I went out onto
the porch with a shotgun in my hands and told
him Mary Helena had changed her mind. She
would not marry him, and she never wanted to see
him again.*

*Thornton refused to believe me, of course, and
demanded to see Mary Helena. I know I was out of*

my mind then. I aimed the shotgun toward him and fired, missing him by no more than a foot. He stood as if frozen and stared at me for a moment. Then he backed to his buckboard, climbed up onto the seat, and left the yard.

I can hardly remember the next few days, but finally it became necessary for me to go into town—I forget why. I admonished the servants to stay away from Mary Helena's room while I was in town. I showed Cinee, the woman who helped us in the house, that I was taking the key to the room with me.

While I was gone, Cinee and the two men who worked in the stables took the hinges off Mary Helena's bedroom door so she could get out. They helped her get some of her things together, and she left with your father.

When I got home, I was mad with anger. I fired all three of them on the spot and ordered them off the place.

Your father must have camped out near the ranch ever since the day I drove him away with the shotgun, waiting for me to leave so he could rescue Mary Helena. He knew that the people who worked on the ranch would probably be more loyal to my sister than they were to me. I was still almost a stranger to them after being away almost five years.

He was certainly right about that. The men were

outraged that I would treat Mary Helena so badly and were glad to help her escape.

I almost killed a good horse riding back to town that day, but I arrived too late. Your mother and father were married earlier in the afternoon, right here in Acorn Creek. I stood in the sitting room of the parsonage and threatened to kill the preacher when I found out he'd performed the ceremony.

I started roaming the woods then, watching them. Thornton knew I was there at times, but I'm sure it was impossible for him to understand how crazed I was. My home was cold and empty. My father was dead and my sister lost to me. Everyone I loved was gone. The loneliness drove me wild.

One afternoon I waited in the woods by the big curve in the road, the one nearest that old dead sycamore. Thornton came around the bend on one of those big brown horses of his. I was elated. I finally had him alone and in my rifle sights.

I swear I could not stop myself. I fired. He fell back in the saddle, lost his grip on the reins, and fell to the ground. At that moment his buckboard came around the curve, with Mary Helena at the reins. She pulled the horses to a stop and jumped down to run to Thornton. She knelt in the muddy road beside him.

Billy Two Horses rode with her. He pulled Thornton's rifle from his saddle boot and slipped into the brush. I could hear him yelling at Mary

Helena to get down before she got shot. She yelled back that Thornton was badly wounded and that Billy should come back and help her get Will into the wagon.

I was horrified at what I had done. I think I woke up at that moment. I believe it happened when I realized Mary Helena was obviously expecting a child. I had almost killed her husband. I had wanted to kill him.

I watched as Billy helped her lift Thornton and settle him in the back of the buckboard. They tied his horse to the tailgate and turned the buckboard around in the road. The last I saw of them, Mary Helena whipped the horses to a run as they took the road back toward town.

Your father lived, of course, and I'm certain he knew exactly who shot him, but not a word was ever said about it in town. I heard people say Thornton put it off on some bushwhacker—told people some drifter figuring to collect his horse and gear shot him, but the man was scared away when he realized Mary Helena and Billy were with him.

Mary Helena came to the ranch to see me three days later. She was driving the buckboard, and Billy Two Horses sat on the seat beside her. He had a double-barrel across his lap. Four men with rifles in their hands rode alongside the buckboard.

She blistered my hide with her words. I know I

*woke up then. I knew she was forever lost to me—
and it was my own fault.*

*When she finished reading me my pedigree and
turned the buckboard to leave, I knew I would
never bother her or Thornton again. I left the
ranch, spending the winter in Guadalajara. That's
where I married Margarita Vargas, Wes' mother.*

*Believe it or not, Red, there is more. I may have
realized I could not control your mother's life, that
I would have to make my own family, but I still carried a lot of hate and resentment for your father.*

*When I came back to White Willow, I found out
that Mary Helena died from influenza when you
were less than a year old. I blamed Thornton for
her death. I swore he failed to protect her, and it
was his fault she got sick. If possible, I managed
to hate your father even more.*

*That's when I committed my worst sin against
your father and you, Red. I refused to probate my
father's will and ignored his wishes about sharing
White Willow with your mother.*

*Your father worked hard to provide for you and
take care of you at the same time. He struggled
through some lean times unnecessarily, because as
Mary Helena's husband, he owned half of White
Willow Ranch and all the other property and con-
siderable money my father left.*

*Later, the hardest thing for me to live with was
your friendship with my son. Wes might never have*

finished school if you had not been there to take his part against other boys and show him your kindness and encouragement. It was exactly what your mother would have done.

I know you used your own savings to bail him out of trouble some years back. I also know you lied to me to keep him out of trouble on more than one occasion.

On top of everything else, I did a worse thing to you than my son ever could have. I knew Wes killed poor Johnny Yates. He never told me he shot the man in so many words, Red, but I'm sure you know as well as I do, it is easy enough to tell when my son is lying.

I knew he killed the man, but I stood by and let you take the blame. I even stood in the back of the courtroom and listened as Judge Sellers sentenced you to years in Yuma prison.

With the help of Doc Bailey, I was able to convince Sheriff Logan that when you shot Johnny, you did not know what you were doing. When he agreed to fix the charge at manslaughter instead of murder, I knew Wes was saved and you would live.

In my selfishness, I told myself you were strong and would make it through five years in Yuma. At my urging, my old friend Judge Sellers agreed to let things unfold as they were and give you the lightest possible sentence.

Please do not hate them for my trickery, Red.

Doc Bailey and Sheriff Logan truly believed you shot Johnny Yates and thought they were helping you. As for Judge Sellers, I have a lot of money, and the man is greedy. He could not resist what I offered.

I did not tell Sellers I believed Wes did the killing. I do honestly believe he thought you guilty of the killing as well, but for what I offered, he was willing for me to convince him you were not responsible for your act at the time.

Red, this has been a long letter, but you needed to know these things. I'm writing this now because I am afraid I will not live long. Gilbert Patten and his gang moved in on the ranch a few weeks ago, and they seem to be getting bolder every day. I'm convinced they will eventually kill me.

I sent Wes south to the ranch down near Guadalajara his mother brought to our marriage. I warned him that if he did not stay there, I would turn him over to the law myself. He left here in the middle of the night without his wife.

Wes married Rebecca McClain the very night he brought her to White Willow. The monsignor from the little chapel over in the Mexican settlement married them. Ben Seymour has a copy of their marriage lines.

Red, I made a new will, leaving you all of White Willow Ranch and a large portion of its earnings for the five good years just past.

I do not know if Wes will ever come back to Acorn Creek, but if he should, show him this letter. He is well provided for, so he has no rights in law to challenge your ownership of the ranch or the money I am leaving you.

Ben Seymour will explain. He drew up the papers. I know White Willow is yours by right, and it's what your mother would have wanted.

Please forgive me, Red,

Your uncle,
John Jacob Lane

Chapter Twelve

Red stared down at the signature on the last page of the letter for a long moment, then closed his eyes. When he raised his head and opened his eyes again, he looked first at the cold cigar in his left hand and then over at Seymour. The lawyer had his head down, poring over some papers and pretending to ignore Red.

Dropping the cigar into the tray on the desk, Red refolded the letter and slid it back into the envelope. Suddenly he pushed the chair back, stood up, and started pacing back and forth across the length of the room as he slapped the thick envelope against his leg.

"Mr. Thornton—Mr. Thornton—Red . . ."

Seymour's voice finally reached him somewhere in the black void the horrible story in the letter had plunged his thoughts into. Red stopped pacing as suddenly as he'd started and whirled around, his face contorted in anger, to face the lawyer as though he was an enemy.

Seymour stood behind his desk, a concerned expression on his face. "I don't know what to say, Mr. Thornton. Is there anything I can do? I thought the letter from Major Lane would be welcome—would be good news. I had no idea it contained information that would upset you so."

"It has nothing to do with you, Mr. Seymour. I'm sorry. I'll calm down. I just couldn't handle it for a few minutes. I'm okay now." Red moved the chair back close to the desk and settled down again. "Before I forget, would you please have that clerk of yours make me a clear copy of this marriage certificate of Wes Lane's?"

"Certainly," Seymour replied.

"You said earlier you had some more papers for me. I'd like to see them now, if you don't mind. They can't be much worse than this letter, and I'd like to get it all over with at once if I can."

"There's certainly nothing in the papers I have here to upset you, Mr. Thornton—Major Lane's will, papers you need to sign to register your deed to the White Willow property, and signature cards you must fill out to assume control of the ranch accounts over at the bank."

"Well, trot them out, and I'll sign them. As I said, I want to get this over with as soon as possible. I have a lot of things to talk over with my father first, and after that, if I'm really the legal owner of White Willow Ranch, I've got a big job ahead of me. That Gilbert Patten and his gang of cutthroat trash hold possession of it at the moment."

"Well, that should be no problem, Mr. Thornton. Sheriff Logan will have to go out there with you and make those crooks clear out. They can't just take over someone's property like that."

"There's two problems with that, Mr. Seymour. First, Sheriff Logan is the town sheriff. He has no authority out there, and Patten surely knows it. Second, Patten has a whole bunch of men holed up out there with him, and every one of them is likely a gunfighter.

"Even if Logan could or would try to help me, I don't know if that gang will leave on his word. They may decide to dig in and make a fight of it. I'm afraid it would take most of an army to get them out by force. I don't know what will happen."

After they reviewed the papers, Seymour collected the necessary copies from John Asbury, put on his hat, and left the office with Red. They walked together to the courthouse to file the papers and then went to the bank to sign more papers to give Red access to the ranch bank accounts.

Red shook his head when he saw the total in the accounts. The major left him well fixed as far as money was concerned, but the knowledge did nothing to help him swallow the lump of anger and bitterness in his throat.

He felt a searing flash of anger cut through his chest every time he thought of his father.

Dad should have told me all of this. I shouldn't have to find out things like this in a letter from my mother's brother. I admired Major Lane. I often bragged to Dad how well the major did at White Willow and urged him to try the same things. I must have sounded like a prime fool to him.

All the time Dad knew this, and he didn't say a word. I can't remember his ever saying a word against the major. 'Course, he never hesitated to say he didn't like Becky McClain, and he certainly made it plain he had no use at all for Wes, but he never said a word about any feud with Major Lane.

I don't know what to do next. I need to talk to Sheriff Logan, but on top of everything, I want to get back up onto the mountain and confront Dad. He's got some tall explaining to do.

That's not all. Billy Two Horses evidently knew what went on as well as Dad did. He's never made any bones about hating Major Lane, but he never told me a thing about why *he hated him. Billy has such violent likes and dislikes, it never occurred to me to push him to tell me why he hated the major so much.*

When Red and Seymour stepped out of the bank, the lawyer turned to hold out his hand. "I'm expecting a client at my office in a few minutes, Mr. Thornton, so I need to get back right away or I'd invite you for a drink.

"Congratulations on your good fortune, sir. Don't hesitate to call on me if I can be of service."

Red almost laughed when Seymour described the last few hours as his "good fortune." Shaking the man's offered hand, he assured Seymour he would continue to handle all the legal work for the ranch.

When the lawyer turned to walk away, Red stood still a few minutes, looking down at the thick letter he still held in his hand. Finally he slid the letter into his inside coat pocket and muttered to himself, "I know what needs doing first."

He walked around the corner beside the courthouse and headed up the hill toward the church, holding the rolled-up copy of Wes and Becky's marriage certificate in one hand. He climbed the stairs and went in the open front door of the church. The sexton stood in the aisle holding a broom.

"Mr. Mills, I'd like to see the preacher."

"Hello there, Thornton. You just missed Reverend Sylvester. He goes home this time of day to eat his dinner. Never misses—no, sir. He's just like clockwork. You daren't bother him now. You'll have to come back here in about an hour. He might see you then."

"Well, how about that? The good reverend has gone home to eat his dinner, has he? Thanks, Mr. Mills. I'll take my chances."

As Red turned to leave, the sexton called after him. "Hold up there, Thornton. I said you can't bother the reverend now. It's one of his rules."

"I heard what you said," Red called over his shoulder. "Thanks for the information."

Red walked back out of the church and down the steps, then skirted around the building and up the steps of the parsonage to rap on the door. After a few moments Mrs. Sylvester opened the door. When she saw who stood in front of her, she pushed the door closed—until it stopped against Red's left boot.

Eyes wide with fright, she squeaked. "What do you want here?"

Red removed his hat. "I want to see Reverend Sylvester, ma'am."

"The reverend's busy."

"I'm sorry, ma'am. This is important. I need to see him now."

"I will not disturb him. He's writing his sermon for this Sunday, and it's almost time for his dinner. He never sees people in his home. He only sees people in his office at the church."

"Well, ma'am, his Sunday sermon is just what I want to see him about. I need to tell him something that will help him with it."

Mrs. Sylvester scowled and pushed against the door again.

Red kept his boot there and grinned down at her.

"You get away from this door, you murderer." The woman's cheeks quivered as she shook her head at Red.

"Go get Reverend Sylvester for me, ma'am. Then I'll gladly leave."

"What is all this?" Reverend Sylvester shouted as he pulled the door wide open. An angry look on his face, he stared at Red. He had removed his coat and was in his shirtsleeves. His tie hung loose, and his collar button was undone.

"I'm sure you remember me, Reverend Sylvester. I'm Rufus Thornton. I have something important to talk to you about."

"I'm really too busy for you right now, Thornton. You should go to my office in the church and make an appointment with my secretary. That's the proper way to do things. I only see people in that office, anyway."

"What I have to say won't wait, Reverend. May I come in?"

"It looks as if you already *are* in young man, so come on into my office."

Reverend Sylvester turned to lead the way down the hall. He entered the second door on the left.

Mrs. Sylvester stood aside with fisted hands resting on her broad hips. She wore an angry scowl and had a hostile expression in her eyes as she watched Red walk down the hall behind her husband.

Reverend Sylvester moved around behind the polished walnut desk that dominated the room, but he did not sit down. "All right, Thornton. What is it you want?"

"I want you to grab your hat and coat and come with me over to Andrew McClain's place, Reverend."

"Jehosephat." The reverend's face flushed with anger.

"Just who do you think you are, young man? I'm a busy man. I have no time to shilly-shally with the likes of you. You're not even a member of my church. Get out of here."

Red placed both hands on the polished surface of the desk and leaned forward to speak softly. "Reverend, it's like this. You're coming with me to the McClains' place, and there's no need for us to do a lot of arguing about it."

"Get out of my house, you cretin."

"I'll go when you get yourself ready to go with me. I don't want to have to pull this .44, but I will if you don't shut up and come along."

"You're crazy."

"That may be, but you're coming with me all the same. You might as well know, I'll do whatever I have to. You're coming with me." Red dropped his hand until his fingers rested on the grip of his pistol.

"Thornton, you're proving you're nothing but a criminal—an out-and-out criminal. When Matthew Sellers hears about this, he is going to be sorry he was so lenient with you for murdering poor old Johnny Yates. This is an outrage. I'll see you sent back to Yuma for this."

Red kept his hand on his pistol and stared at the minister.

Still sputtering, Reverend Sylvester straightened his tie, secured the gold pin at his throat, and pulled on his black coat. Taking his hat down from the rack, he stepped around Red and out into the hall, slamming the hat down so far, it made his ears stick out.

"Millie, I'm going out for a while. Don't wait dinner for me."

Wrapped in a white apron, Mrs. Sylvester came out of a door farther along the hall, a distressed expression on her face. Her whole body stiffened as she whined, "But, Reverend, your dinner is almost ready—you have to eat."

"Don't fuss, woman. I'll be back as soon as I can."

"But you never let anything interfere with your dinner."

"I have to go out, woman. I'll explain later."

Reverend Sylvester, with Red a few steps behind, left Millie Sylvester standing at the open front door of the parsonage, staring after them.

Red stayed a little behind the preacher as they walked up the street. He kept one hand casually resting on the grip of his pistol and held the rolled-up marriage certificate in the other. Reverend Sylvester cut his eyes toward him every few steps, as if hoping he would disappear.

When they reached the door of Andrew McClain's café, Red reached around Reverend Sylvester's bulk to push it open wide.

"Go ahead on in, Reverend. I'll be right behind you."

"I want to know what you think you're doing," Reverend Sylvester said over his shoulder as he stepped inside. "I have a right to know what's going on here."

Most of the café tables were full of customers eating

their dinner. Andrew McClain stood behind the counter, his hands in a dishpan, his back to the door. Jeannie stopped pouring coffee and stared.

Giving the reverend a little shove in the direction of the counter, Red followed the big man across the room and sat down on the only empty stool. Turning to face the room, he slipped his pistol out of his holster and held it in his lap.

Raising his voice, Red said, "Don't be alarmed, folks. I'm sorry to interrupt your dinner, but the good reverend here is going to read you this paper I'm holding.

"He's going to read it out nice and loud so everybody can hear what it says. When he finishes reading it, he's gonna get down on his knees and beg somebody's forgiveness."

The crowded room fell silent.

Reverend Sylvester's face flushed with anger, and his voice came out at a sharp pitch, showing his fear and indignation, when he shouted, "You're crazy, Thornton! You're as crazy as a loon!"

"That may well be true, Reverend. I've been through enough lately to make anybody act a little crazy. But you're going to do what I say and hurry up about it. Make up your mind to it—you're gonna preach your sermon this Sunday with a bandage covering the place where your right ear is supposed to be if you don't unroll this paper and read it out loud like I said."

The preacher took the paper and unrolled it. He quickly scanned the contents. When he looked back up at Red, his face was white. Seeing the stern expression on Red's face, he then turned slightly to see the hatred on the face of Andrew McClain.

His voice small, Sylvester barely whispered, "My stars, Thornton. Please. I had no idea about this. There is no way I could have known this."

"Don't talk about it—read it out loud, blast you."

Swallowing hard, Reverend Sylvester removed his hat and spread the paper out on the counter and read aloud:

"Know all men by these presents: John Wesley Lane and Rebecca Lynn McClain are joined in Holy Matrimony this twenty-seventh day of February 1887."

He stopped reading to look across the room at the interested faces of the crowd. "This is signed by Monsignor Xavier Luis Reyes-Orlando of Grace Mission."

Sweat dripped from Reverend Sylvester's forehead, and his voice rose an octave higher. "You must believe me, Mr. McClain, I had no idea. I didn't know about this. Someone should have told me."

McClain started to reach across the counter, his hands poised to grab the preacher, his fingers like claws, but Red reached out and pushed him back. "Take it easy, McClain. I'm not finished."

Turning back to face Reverend Sylvester, Red wrapped his free hand around the grip of his .44 and lifted it a few inches as he said, "Get down on your knees, preacher."

"No—I won't do it. Thornton, this is crazy. I didn't know about this marriage—there was no way for me to know about it."

"That's just the point, preacher. You didn't know. But not knowing, you still had the meanness to refuse to bury Becky in church ground or preach a sermon over her to give comfort to her relatives.

"Not only that, you and your wife, along with that pack of old biddies at the church, have done all you could to ruin Jeannie McClain's reputation for no more than being good enough to care for her nephew.

"On top of everything, you've named that innocent baby of Becky's a bastard to everyone who would listen, whether they were interested or not. Much of the damage you've done here can never be undone.

"Get down on your knees, you sorry imitation of a pastor. Move—I'm plumb out of patience with you."

Red stood up and gave Reverend Sylvester a push.

Sylvester held on to the front edge of the counter with both hands as he slid down to his knees. His face chalky white and dripping sweat, he dropped his forehead against the skirting around the counter and almost sobbed as he pleaded, "Please forgive me. I didn't know—I didn't know."

Red yelled, "Say it louder, so everybody can hear you!"

The front door of the café slammed open. Leon

Jackson strode in with his hand on his pistol, shouting, "What the dickens is going on here? What devilment are you up to now, Red Thornton?

"Reverend Sylvester's poor wife came running into my office a minute ago, crying her eyes out and near scared to death. She said you forced your way into the parsonage and kidnapped the reverend at gunpoint."

Red grinned as he held up both hands. He had slipped his pistol back into its holster as soon as Reverend Sylvester's knees hit the floor. "Well, now, Leon, that's about as silly a thing as I ever heard anybody say. The good reverend here is just praying with these folks for the pure soul of sweet little Becky McClain. Ain't that the right of it, Reverend?"

Reverend Sylvester pulled himself to a standing position and sputtered something unintelligible as he stared at Red's holstered pistol.

"You see, Leon?" Red continued. "The good reverend is speechless at your notion that I kidnapped him—and at gunpoint, no less."

"What the heck is going on here?" Leon frowned as he looked from Red to Reverend Sylvester.

"Never you mind, Leon," Reverend Sylvester said as he grabbed his hat and started for the door. He turned back—twice—to look at Red as he stopped to tell Leon that his wife was easily frightened, often mistook the truth of things, and became excited over nothing.

Jeannie came over to Red, took his arm, and pulled it close to her side. Her blue eyes swam with tears.

"Thank you, Red. Thank you. Words sound so feeble—I don't know what else to say. Look at Dad. I've never seen tears in his eyes before. Not even when poor Becky died."

Andrew McClain spread his daughter's marriage certificate out on the counter and stared down at it.

Red looked down at the dark hair almost touching his shoulder. He could smell roses. He gently eased his arm away from Jeannie's. He could feel his face flaming. Her touch seemed to burn his arm through his jacket and shirt.

I need to get outside where I can breathe.

"It's all right now, Jeannie. Tell your dad I'll come back to town in a few days and explain all I know about this."

"Stay with us now, Red." Jeannie looked up, her eyes pleading. "I know Dad will want to thank you for doing this for us. You've never even met little Joseph, either. Please stay."

"I can't, Jeannie. I have to get up to Chief Billy's place. I'll come for supper one night soon."

"You're always welcome, Red. You know that."

"I know. Maybe your dad won't scowl at me so much now."

"Oh, Red. You know he won't. He'd better not, anyway. He'll hear from me if he does."

Chapter Thirteen

Everything seemed quiet when Red rode into the open space between the barn and Billy's cabin. He unsaddled Pitch and led him into a stall that opened into the pasture. Piling sweet hay in the manger, he poured a small amount of grain into one corner and dipped a bucket of fresh water from the trough.

While Pitch ate, Red took the time to brush the horse thoroughly, paying a lot of attention to smoothing the hair on his back. When he finished, he checked the animal's feet carefully before he left for the cabin.

"I've delayed this long enough," he muttered to himself as he walked across the yard. "I'm still mad enough to spit, but I think I can talk about Mother without losing my temper."

Will Thornton lay on his bunk, reading.

"Where's Billy, Dad?"

"He went over to his sister's place early this morning. He got up acting sort of mysterious. I don't know just what he's up to."

"Well, since he's gone, I've got some things I need to talk to you about."

"You sound serious, son."

"I am. Serious enough that I think I'd like to go ahead and eat some supper first if that's all right with you."

"There's some son-of-a-gun stew on the back of the stove. Get us a bucket of cold water, and I'll get the food onto the table."

Red and his father hardly spoke during the meal.

As soon as his father put down his spoon, Red looked up and said, "First off, what's the deal with you and John Wallace Barrone? Why would he dislike you so much, he finds it necessary to take jabs at me?"

"Barrone's a jealous fool. Years ago he and I had a fight. It was a fair fight, and I won. That's all there is to it."

"What did you fight about?"

Will Thornton studied his son's face for a moment before he answered, lowering his eyes. "I'm not proud of it, son. Barrone and I fought because I refused to drink with him."

"That doesn't sound like you. Why in the world would you refuse to drink with him?"

"That was a lie made out of the truth, son." Will ran one hand through his hair and resettled himself in his chair. "I didn't just refuse to drink with the man. I didn't want to tell you the truth. Barrone and I fought over a woman. It was about two years after your mother died. You remember when I made regular trips over to the reservation on business?"

"I always wondered what that 'business' of yours was."

"Well, now you know, so I'll get back to my story.

"Barrone thinks he should be able to rule every person who lives on that reservation—he always has. I refused to drink with him after he tried to stop a woman there from seeing me.

"He tried everything he could to make her stop. He told her father she was in danger, that I would mistreat her, that I had a reputation of beating women. When that didn't work, he started meeting her on the road every time she went anywhere alone and hounding her to marry his brother.

"He did everything he could to make her stop seeing me, and when she wouldn't stop, he finally came to her house one day when I was there.

"Barrone could plainly see my horse tied up at her gatepost. She went to the door when he knocked, and I followed. I stood right behind her when she opened it. He stood there in the doorway and called her a dirty squaw to her face. He wore that superior-looking grin on his face when he said it, and it made me so mad, I lit into him.

"His brother was with him and tried to grab me from behind, but the woman pointed my rifle at him, bless her heart, and held him off while I fought Barrone.

The man could fight, Indian style, but I had some reach on him, and I know a little about boxing. His brother had to help him onto his horse so he could get home.

We did a rematch in the store down at Benton when I refused to have a drink and 'forget our differences,' as he put it."

"I can see how Barrone would hold that against you. Thanks for telling me about it."

"I reckon Billy didn't want to tell you because he thought you might have a problem with my seeing someone after your mother."

"Well, that's pretty silly. He could have told me— I'm not that foolish."

Red looked down at the table for a moment, then lifted his head and looked directly at his father. "There's something else I need to ask you about, Dad. I went to see Ben Seymour today. He gave me a letter from Major Lane. It told me a lot of things I needed to know about my mother, but there's still a lot you should tell me."

Red took a deep breath before continuing. "To be frank, I'm not a bit happy I learned these things from Major Lane, and I'm even less happy that I learned them at such a late date."

"What are you saying, son?"

"Will you tell me why you avoided Major Lane all these years and why you never told me anything about why you avoided him?"

Will Thornton lowered his head to stare at his plate.

After a long moment he lifted his head and looked into Red's eyes.

"I'm sorry, son. I've set out to tell you all this a hundred times at least. I've never spoken of it since it happened. When she was dying, your mother begged me over and over to mend fences with her brother. She was so sick, and almost the last thing she told me was to please forgive John and make sure you got to know him as you grew up. She lay there on that bed so weak, she couldn't lift a hand, and she begged me.

"I couldn't do it. Even after she begged me, I just couldn't do it, son. I resented everything John Lane did so much, I couldn't get over it. I felt—I think I felt completely broken after your mother died," Will admitted.

"But, Dad, I still can't understand why you wouldn't tell me about any of these things. I'm sorry, but I think I was entitled to know. I'm afraid I'm sitting here resenting the fact that I found these things out in a letter from the major."

Will was scowling. His gnarled hands were balled into fists, one lying on each side of his plate.

"Lane had no right to tell you anything. That man never had a lick of sense. I don't see how he thought he had a right to tell you anything about your mother after the things he did."

Red took the leather pouch holding Major John Lane's letter out of his pocket and tossed it across the table.

"Read the letter, Dad. I think you'll understand then.

I'll go check on the foals. Give me a yell when you're finished."

Leaving the house, Red walked over to the paddock fence and leaned on the top rail. He couldn't keep his thoughts on the horses; everything he had learned that day swirled through his mind.

What can I do about Gilbert Patten? All I can think of to do about him and that low-down crew of his is to go back into town in a day or two and put it to Sheriff Logan to help me find a solution. Maybe he can call in some law with enough authority to clear those skunks out of White Willow. Surely a marshal is coming to find out who murdered the man Barrone found.

If I go back over there—even if I go like Billy and I did before—I'll either get myself killed, or they'll burn the place down to keep me from getting it.

I want that house, now that I know it's mine. It has at least two bedrooms on the bottom floor, and it's made out of those big old logs. It'd be perfect for Dad with his rheumatism. That is, it'd be perfect if I could ever get him to go there.

It would be much more comfortable for him than our house. I know Dad loves the ranch, but the house is made of boards, and the bedrooms are all upstairs. Billy was right about its being cold too. The wind can find the way inside that house in at least a hundred places.

Dad's sure stubborn enough to refuse to go even if I figure out a way to get Patten and his crew out. He knew

*all these years that half of White Willow Ranch was his
by right through my mother, and he completely ignored
it. Plain and simple, he sat there on our little ranch and
ignored it.*

Pushing himself away from the fence, Red turned to
walk back to the cabin. When he entered, his father
still sat at the table, his head now resting on his folded
arms.

Red took a chair without speaking.

Will raised his head and met his eyes. "I can hardly
believe this, son. That sorry so-and-so knew you were
innocent, and he still let those devils send you to that
awful place. I never knew anyone—even John Lane—
could be so low-down. He plain out stole almost three
years of your life. I'm glad the sorry sneak is dead, and
I hope that miserable son of his is too."

"Calm down, Dad. Don't upset yourself about that. I
already went over what I'd like to do to Major Lane,
Wes, Judge Sellers, and everybody else concerned for
doing me that way. I got a lot of it out of me straightening out that sorry excuse of a preacher for what he did
about poor Becky McClain and her baby."

Red shook his head in remembered anger. "I still got
so het up thinking about it while I was riding up here, I
forgot and spurred Pitch. He like to threw me in the
middle of the road. I couldn't do a thing but laugh at
myself.

"Just forget it, Dad. That's what I'm gonna do. I'm
going to forget it until I can find a way to prove I'm

innocent. There's no profit in either one of us sitting around stewing over it," Red concluded.

"It's just so sorry and low-down. It makes my stomach ache," Will said. "I knew it of Wes. I always expected him to find a way to do you dirt. I warned you a hundred times to stay away from him. But for John Lane, your mother's brother—for him to know you were innocent, yet let such a thing happen to you to protect his own son? I can't get over the malice of it."

"Tell me more about the things the major said about Mother in the letter."

"I know I should have told you, son. I'm sorry. You've always been so content, even when you were a little kid. Then when you took to looking after Wes all the time, keeping him out of trouble at school and with his father, I decided you didn't need to hear old news.

"As for your mother's part of White Willow Ranch, she wouldn't let me ask for it when she was alive, so I wouldn't ask for it later. I guess it sort of laid the way open for me to keep on hating John Lane. I sure wanted to. I guess it might have helped me some for him to keep it—with me knowing he wasn't entitled to it.

"I have to admit, I can't help but feel a little ashamed of myself for it after reading his letter. Keeping the ranch away from me didn't make him one bit happy, that's for sure. And it didn't help you any, either."

"You're right there, Dad. The major certainly wasn't

a happy man when he wrote that letter. I'd go so far as to say he'd given up, don't you think?"

"He was looking for some grace when he deeded White Willow to you. He was like an old man who'd lived a wicked life trying to buy his way into heaven.

"Say, I just thought of something, son. What are you going to do about that Patten and his bunch of cut-throats squatting over at White Willow? You'll have to find a way to get rid of them before you can take over the ranch."

"I know that, Dad. I've been thinking about it. I'll go to the law about that. I hate to have to do it—a man ought to be able to take care of his own trouble—but I want to be careful. If I push too hard, those owl-hoots will get back at me some way. I don't want them to burn the place down to keep me from getting it.

"But stop trying to change the subject. You're sup-posed to be telling me about those things in Major Lane's letter about you and Mother."

"There's not a whole lot more to tell. Lane covered it pretty well. He came home from the War about half dead. Something was wrong with his chest, and I reckon there was something wrong with his head as well. All he wanted was for things to be exactly like they were when he left, but that was impossible.

"John couldn't accept the fact that his little Mary He-lena grew up while he was gone. It was as if he wanted to force her to be his baby sister again, same as she was when he left home.

"All those things happened just as he said in his letter. When he ran me off with his shotgun that day, I made out like I left, but I circled around and stayed in the woods along the creek that runs down the hill behind the house.

"Later, I sneaked through the woods and into the bunkhouse to talk to a couple of the old hands. They'd worked on the ranch most of your mother's life. They already knew from that Indian woman about John's locking Mary Helena in her room and not letting her out. They were furious with him. Anyway, they promised to help me get her away from there. They said the Indian woman would help too.

"John finally rode to town on some sort of business. As soon as he left the ranch, those two men and the Indian woman and I took her door off the hinges and got Mary Helena out of her room. She packed up some of her things, and we left there together.

"Your mother rode double with me until we got over to the Sanders' place. You know where that is, way over to the east side of Acorn Creek. We explained what all had happened, and Rich Sanders rode into town right then to tell the preacher what was going on. We got to town a few hours later, and he married your mother and me that very night. It wasn't that puffed-up toad of a preacher we've got now. It was an older man.

"We went back to the Sanders ranch and stayed that night. The next day Mary Helena and I went home—to our place. We figured once we were married, John would get himself straightened out—he would have to.

"Well, it didn't work out that way. John commenced to watch us. I knew it for a long time before I ever let your mother know he did it. He got a little crazy, I guess. He never came to the house or barns, but I caught glimpses of him in the woods or way off from the road, watching us through a glass.

"It never occurred to me I was in any real danger from him even after he'd shot at me with the shotgun that day. Billy kept telling me I was, that John was looking to kill me, but your mother and I couldn't believe he would actually hurt one of us.

"Billy begged me to let him kill John. Of course, I told him no. With all his faults, your mother loved her brother. I think that's the worst thing of all. John Lane forgot how much his sister loved him."

"I don't know how she could keep on loving him after all that," Red observed.

"You think about it some, son. You've forgiven Wes for his meanness more times than you can count over the years. You've got your mother's kind heart. I've got a feeling you're well on the way to forgiving him for branding you a murderer and making you serve almost three years in prison."

"I don't know about that. If it hadn't been for the major's being friends with Judge Sellers and Doc Bailey's swearing I was out of my head when Johnny Yates was killed, I coulda been hanged for the man's murder. I'm not so sure I'll be able to forgive Wes for all that too easily."

"Well, to get back to my story, Billy was so undone with us after John shot me that day, he was ready to kill him. I wouldn't let him do anything about it except ride over there with your mother so she could tell John what she thought of him.

"The incident upset Billy so much, he went off and left us for a while. He went back over the mountain and stayed with his sister—that little one called Willie Mae—for more than a year. I wasn't sure there for a while if he would ever come back.

"When your mother got sick, he heard about it and rode into the yard one day. I don't know what I would have done if he hadn't been there when she died. Like I told you before, I got a little crazy for a while. Billy rode into town and got the preacher to come out and took care of everything.

"He got Mrs. Sanders' youngest daughter to come over to the ranch and tend you for a day or two while he rode back over to where his sister lives and brought Ramona to live at the ranch and take care of you."

"When I was little, I used to pretend Ramona was really my mother. I think I was a little angry with Mother for dying on me."

"That's an odd thing, isn't it? I felt like that a few times myself. I was mad at the world for a long time. I finally got over it, though. You can't live on hate for long. It eats at you until you can't enjoy anything.

"I guess it was when you got big enough to ride out with me regular that I sort of woke up. All of a sudden I realized I had the best friend in the world in Chief Billy Two Horses, a fine young son, and a housekeeper who took perfect care of us. It hit me hard to realize I was acting downright ungrateful not to appreciate all of you any more than I did. Things got better for me then."

"You never thought about owning part of White Willow? I can remember several times when we got down to scraping the bottom of the barrel as far as money goes. Didn't you think about going after what you were entitled to then—when you needed something to help us get along?"

"I know—but I told you earlier. Every time I thought of saying something to Lane about it or going to the law to get it, I remembered your mother's telling me to leave it—that it wasn't worth fighting her brother over. I knew she never would have changed, no matter what, so I just left it.

"You always had a roof over your head and plenty of food. You even rode a good horse almost from the time you could walk. What did you want for that you didn't have?"

"Not a doggone thing when it comes down to it. I just thought lack of money was awful hard on you sometimes."

"Hey. I hear a horse. I hope that's Billy coming back."

"I hear it. If it is Billy, I'm going into town tomorrow. Sheriff Logan is supposed to be back by then, and I want to talk to him about what I can do about Gilbert Patten and his bunch of shooters sitting over there at White Willow."

Chapter Fourteen

Red felt different the next morning when he rode into Acron Creek. It was early, and the day looked like it might just shape up to be a nice one. Pitch's shoes ringing on the oak boards of the bridge seemed cheerful— they almost made a happy sound.

Maybe I am getting over Wes and the whole mess of the last three years. Dad's probably right—staying mad forever could sour somebody's whole life.

I reckon things really are looking up—a little. I made it all the way to the sheriff's office without meeting a single soul who stopped and stared at me as if I were a monster or turned his back on me. Maybe some people are getting over hating me for Johnny Yates' killing.

Tying Pitch to the rail in front of the building, he opened the door and walked into Sheriff Logan's office. Logan sat behind his desk writing. He nodded to Red without speaking.

"I've a letter here from Major Lane, Sheriff Logan. I'd be obliged if you'd read it. It's long, but it says some important things you need to know."

"Sure, I'll read it, Red. Leave it, and come back in about an hour. I'm working on some things here, and I have to get 'em finished right away."

"If you don't mind, Logan, I'd sort of like to sit down here and wait. This letter is a mighty precious document to me."

"Well, sure thing, Red. You can certainly wait. I've just got to finish writing out these telegrams and get them off as soon as I can." The sheriff looked closely at him. "By the way, I understand from Leon that you had another real important document for the McClains the other day."

"You've got that right."

"Leon said Reverend Sylvester acted out-and-out strange that day. What in the world was all that about?"

"It was nothing at all, Logan. Nothing at all. It seems to me that Reverend Sylvester acts a little strange most of the time. At least he does from what I've heard Dad and Billy say about him and what I observed the other day. I couldn't help but notice how much his ears stick out, though. He looks right comical with that black hat pushed down on his head."

"Well, I went over to the café, and Andrew McClain let me see his daughter's marriage certificate, so I've been passing the word to everybody I can get to listen.

"I been thinking a lot of folks in this town owe Jeannie McClain an apology. I'm almost ashamed to say it, but I've been forced to speak to three different men about the way they acted around her in the last two years. Leon Jackson, my own deputy, was one of them.

"Those fellas took a notion into their heads that if Becky McClain was a bad girl—and the reverend kept on yammering about how bad she was—then her little sister was surely bad as well. Reverend Sylvester has a lot to answer for, it seems to me."

"That poor man was so upset when he read that marriage certificate that he went down on his knees and begged the McClains' pardon." Red was grinning as he spoke.

"Yeah. I believe that, Red—sure I do. A couple of fellas who were in the café that day claim they saw your .44 lying in your lap while you were sitting up there at the counter next to Sylvester. Say, what was all that rigamarole about his ears all about anyway? Did Leon miss something?"

"I guess he must have, Sheriff Logan. Remember— Leon's a little dense sometimes. Reverend Sylvester somehow seemed very concerned about keeping his ears attached to his head."

"I figured it was gonna be something like that. Mrs. Sylvester came in here crying and screaming, telling Leon you were threatening her husband. You need to kinda soft-pedal that sort of thing Red—if you don't mind too much. Not that I can personally disagree with anything you did."

Sheriff Logan gathered up several sheets of paper and stood. "I'll run these over to Matthews at the telegraph office and come right back. You can wait there if you want. I won't be but a minute or two. I'm eager to see what's in that letter you set so much store by."

Logan folded the letter and slid it back into the leather pouch. "I can't hardly believe this. I always admired the major. I had it in my head he was somebody to look up to. That man knew you were innocent of Johnny Yates' murder, yet he stood by and watched while you went to trial, got convicted, and went to prison. Of all the low-down, sorry, good-for-nothing somebodies, he about takes the cake. Like I said, I can't hardly believe it."

"I've had my problems with it, Logan, but the man's dead, and Wes is beyond reach for now, and that's probably a good thing. What I need now is some help claiming White Willow Ranch. Gilbert Patten and his cronies are still holed up there."

"I heard that, Red, but I'm the Acorn Creek town sheriff—you know that as good as I do. This badge don't mean a thing way out there."

"I know that, of course, but didn't you send for a U.S. Marshal to come investigate that other marshal's murder? It'll take an army to get those crooks out of there unless I can figure some way to get a bunch of men together and sneak up on them. If we try to get them out and fail, it would be just like Patten to fire the place to keep me from getting it. That's what I'm worried about."

"Why couldn't the marshal lead a posse right in there and take over?"

"Patten's got the place guarded. Billy and me went up there the other day. Some of Patten's men helped themselves to my two-year-olds and some yearlings, about ten head in all. We rode up there, and old Billy warned me to look before I rode out into the open.

"Sure enough, when we got up close, we could see two armed guards sitting their horses just inside the main gate to the ranch. Well, to make a long story short, we got the drop on them and sent Patten a message.

"I told those fellas to tell Patten about the brand I put on all of Pitch's foals. It's hidden up under their manes. All they had to do was catch one of them and check what I said. I use a tiny iron and brand them with my initials followed by a number. I didn't want to disfigure them with a regular brand, but I wanted to keep them safe.

"Every one of those horses has got my initials and a number under its mane, and the brand is registered down here at the courthouse. I told the men to remind Patten that horse-stealing is still a hanging offense in this part of Arizona Territory, and it's always of interest to a United States Marshal.

"I didn't know then that I was going to end up owning the place. But I told those fellas guarding the gate to tell Patten that all I wanted was my horses back. It worked too. They were back in Chief Billy's pasture, none the worse for wear, the very next day.

"Those two guards are still there by the front gate, though. I'll bet there's two more at the gate over near Jeston's place and some down by the river where Lane kept his flatboat."

Logan stood up and started to pace back and forth across the office. "I hope to get a deputy marshal up here. That's what some of the telegrams I just sent were about. There's been a bunch of robberies and killings around. I hadn't thought much about its maybe having something to do with Patten and his bunch, because every one of them was more than a day's ride away, but maybe I'd better start thinking.

"It could be them owl-hoots of Patten's are doing their meanness and then coming back here to hide out. I'm gonna send a wire suggesting that to the marshal's office down to Yuma. It can't hurt none. Truth be known, it's what that dead marshal was investigating up at Glade Spring. Are you and Thorn still staying over to Billy Two Horses' cabin, Red?"

"We are. We may stay on there until the weather warms up good. Our house is as cold as a mountain creek, and Dad is bothered with rheumatism something fierce. Billy's got that cabin of his so tight, he can warm it up until you need to go outside to cool off every so often.

"We drove all our cattle up into the hills three years

ago when I went down to Yuma. We were seriously low on cash then. Dad had just paid to have those two new wells drilled over on the west acreage. It left us strapped.

"I was all set to do some work for Major Lane. It would have made me enough money to see us through the winter. That was just before I went to jail.

"When I couldn't get the money we needed, Dad and Billy gave the two men working for us their time. They set in and drove the whole herd of cattle up into those little hollows where they'd have plenty of feed to make it through a normal winter even if we got a lot of snow. I'd been cutting and stacking a lot of feed through the summer, so I was sure they would make it through all right.

"Billy and Dad checked on the cattle now and again. He says too many were killed the first year, and he and Dad shot a mort of wolves up there. I guess a lot of them were preying on the herd.

"Last winter and the one before, Dad and Billy made a deal with one of those Indian friends of Billy's down near the reservation to winter the cattle on his extra pasture. They moved them up top for summer pasture last summer. We were over there, getting ready to move the herd up to the high pastures for this summer, when Barrone brought me that marshal's body.

"We're going to do a gather and sell about fifty head of adult stuff. We'll be able to get us a crew and bring the herd back down to the ranch, now that we have a little money to pay hands and buy supplies."

"Why did you chase the cows up onto the mountain that time? Why didn't you move them over to Billy's place?"

"Chief Billy doesn't really have enough grass on his place for a herd of cattle. His place is small. His biggest pasture backs right up to part of White Willow, you know. And if they'd stayed down on our range, every single one would have been rustled with nobody there to watch them.

"Billy and Dad knew they had to do a good job of taking care of Dad's Belgian horses and my mustang crosses. They're really our future.

"That's why I branded those foals of mine like I did. Dad has always done it with those big horses he raises, and he showed me how. We're gonna raise and sell those horses for a living instead of spending the rest of our lives fighting with all the trouble of raising cattle for the market."

"You'll likely have to change your mind now. White Willow is certainly a cattle ranch—always has been."

"I've got a feeling it might not be so much of one by the time we get that bunch of Patten's out of there."

"What do you mean by that? Do you think they're driving the White Willow cattle somewhere and selling them?"

"They're bound to be, Logan. They've got to get money to live on from somewhere. Unless they really are leaving White Willow now and again to rob banks and stages and coming back there to hide, like you said."

"That's always possible. I'll send a telegram to my friend Deputy Marshal Phillip Glover and ask if he thinks a gang like Patten's mighta done those robberies and made it all the way back here to White Willow to hide out.

"Seems to me I've heard stories of a gang of outlaws operating in this valley before Acorn Creek was ever settled. If he thinks there could be anything to the idea, it'll bring him here running. I'll write out the telegram right now and send it today."

Logan stood up and reached across the desk to hold out his hand, a concerned expression on his face. "Red, I'm downright troubled about what was done to you. I have to admit I had my doubts when it all happened, but I couldn't do nothing but go with the evidence put in front of me.

"In hindsight, I knew and so did a lot of people that Wes Lane was prone to tell stories—stories to always make everything light on himself. I hope you can overlook my part in it."

"It's done, Logan," Red said, shaking the sheriff's hand. "I can't say I'll forget my time in prison, but there's nothing anybody can do to make it any better right now. Just listen hard when somebody tells you they're innocent, and remember, every now and again a body just might be telling you the truth."

"I'll never forget that—you can bet on it. I'll settle my mind completely before I get up in court and accuse anybody of anything again."

"That's all anybody can ask, Logan, and thank you." Red settled his hat onto his head and waved at Logan as he tucked the leather pouch back into his pocket and left the office.

Chapter Fifteen

Chief Billy was at home when Red reached the cabin. He'd ridden in late the night before and went straight to his bed in the loft without letting Red or Will know he was there. Ramona and another Indian woman were there as well; they arrived while Red was in town.

Billy, the two women, and Will waited on the porch while Red finished stabling Pitch and came out of the barn.

Ramona ran across the yard to hug Red and smiled with delight when he kissed her cheek. She laughed aloud and patted his chest and arms as if checking to see if he was all there.

Billy introduced the second woman as Emma Morgan. She stayed close to Billy but smiled and said hello to Red in perfect English. Although obviously Indian, with smooth black hair and shining black eyes, both women wore stylish riding skirts with matching short jackets and polished boots.

Hmm—this looks kind of interesting. I wonder how many of these visits happened while I was away from home?

As Red watched the two women, it became obvious that Ramona stayed as close to his father as the other woman did to Chief Billy.

I think it might be a good thing if I could find a reason to leave and give these people some privacy.

"Dad, I think we ought to ride down to our house early tomorrow and see how things look around the old place. Maybe we could spend a few hours getting the house ready for us to move back into pretty soon."

Billy suddenly seemed to grow a foot taller. He walked over to stand in front of Red, his face flushed and his voice a little high pitched, "No, Red. That's why Ramona and Emma came back here with me. We plan to go down to the house tomorrow ourselves. These women will clean and prepare the house for you and Thorn to return to as soon as it gets warm enough. You can't go. You and your father must stay here to guard the horses and take care of them."

Straining to keep a grin from breaking across his face, Red shrugged and said, "That's okay with me, Billy. If that's what you want to do, you go right ahead. It really makes no never-mind to me."

"Hey, wait a minute, you two." Will stepped off the porch and walked over to join them. "I can still decide for myself what I want to do. I don't need my own son and an old broken-down Indian bronc rider telling me how to live."

"Well, excuse me, Thorn. I thought you told me you needed to explain Ramona and Emma to Red before they stayed here with us again."

Will's face flushed, and he leaned close to Billy's face. "For Pete's sake, Billy. Can't you shut up? I haven't gotten a chance to talk to Red about it yet, and you know blame well I haven't."

"Oh? Well, excuse me. I'm just an old broken-down Indian bronc rider. What could I know?"

"You sorry old son-of-a-gun. I'll tell him right now."

Will turned to face Red, reaching out to take Ramona's hand at the same time. "Ramona and me are gonna be married, son. We would have been hitched already, except that fat so-called preacher down to Acorn Creek flat-out refused to perform the ceremony.

"Sylvester claimed he didn't hold with whites marrying Indians. Not satisfied with that, he wouldn't marry Billy and Emma either. He said Indians were nothing but savages and wouldn't understand the meaning of the Christian ceremony at all.

"Anyway, we're waiting for Father Orlando to come

through here again. We left word at all the ranches where he usually stops for him to come up here or send somebody to let us know when he's around."

Red shook his head and reached out to lay a hand on his father's shoulder. "That Reverend Sylvester has a lot to answer for, doesn't he? I shoulda shot off both his ears just for good measure."

"Shot off Reverend Sylvester's ears? What in the name of goodness are you talking about, son?"

"Never mind about Reverend Sylvester, Dad. I'm glad Ramona finally decided to make an honest man of you."

Red laughed out loud as an expression of astonishment flew across his father's face. "Dad, do you actually think I'm too thickheaded to see how you and Ramona feel about each other?"

"I guess it never occurred to me you knew, son. When I first started noticing Ramona, she was so young, I was downright ashamed of the way I felt. But when you started school, and Ramona and me were left alone all day, it just sort of happened. I always thought we hid it from you, though."

"I've always known, and I'm glad for you, Dad. You know I love Ramona. I'll be proud to call her Mother if she wants me to."

"Thank you, son. I feel a heap better now that it's all out in the open."

Pushing his hat back, Will stared at the expression of

delight on Red's face. "You can stop laughing like a hyena if you don't mind. I'm glad I don't have to hide anymore. Does that suit you?"

Turning to look over at Billy's happy grin, Will continued, "You can wipe that silly grin off your face too, you weasel."

Billy raised both hands and looked serious as he said, "Stop laughing, everybody. I hear a horse out on the road, and it sounds like it's running flat-out."

The whole group turned to watch where the lane curved around the barn and entered the yard. The rider leaned over the horse's neck, swinging a quirt, hitting the horse with every bound.

"It's Jeannie McClain pushing her horse like that," Red said. "What in the world? What's happened now?"

Jeannie slid down from the saddle. Her hair was loose, falling wildly around her face. She was trembling so hard, she leaned forward against Red's chest as he reached to put his arms around her.

"They took him, Red. They took baby Joseph." She sobbed aloud around the words.

"What are you saying, girl? They took the baby? Who?" He took her shoulders in both hands and pushed her back. "Stop crying, so I can understand what you say."

Jeannie wiped her face on a sleeve of her coat and held her head up to speak clearly. "It was Gilbert Patten and three of his men. They came into the café and ate their dinner. After they finished, they paid their bill and left. About an hour later they came back. I was cleaning up the tables, and Dad was in the back, washing dishes. I opened the door to the house as usual after we close, so the baby could toddle around the café while I worked.

"Patten and three of his men walked in. He didn't say a word, and neither did any of his men. He gave me a hard look, moved straight over to where Joey was playing, picked him up, and walked out the front door.

"I was too astonished and scared to move for a second. Then I started screaming and rushed outside after them. By the time I got through the door, they were on their horses and riding away.

"I ran down to the sheriff's office, but Logan and Leon Jackson are both out somewhere—nobody knows where they went. I didn't know what else to do—so here I am. You've got to help me, Red. You've got to help me get Joey back."

"We'll do something, Jeannie. But what I can't figure out is, why in the name of goodness would Patten do such a thing?"

"I searched my brain all the way up here. All I can figure is there's been some talk around town about your inheriting White Willow Ranch. Patten must think he can use Joseph somehow to keep control of the ranch. I can't think of anything else."

"I don't know what to tell you. Come on into the

house, Jeannie. You're exhausted. Come on in. We'll figure out something."

She dropped her head against Red's chest and wailed, "Oh, Red! He's so little! He'll be scared to death!"

"Calm down, honey. They won't hurt the boy. We'll find out soon enough what Patten wants."

One arm clasped around Jeannie's shoulders, Red motioned to Billy. "Put her horse away, and saddle a horse for yourself, Billy. Ride into town and find the sheriff. We've got to have help with this.

"Be sure to stop by and see if Andrew McClain has gotten any kind of ransom note. Make sure he understands he should let us know immediately if he hears anything from Patten. Tell him Jeannie is here and safe."

Billy scowled at Red and turned to Emma. "Get your pack, and come with me. We will follow this one's orders, and then we'll go to prepare Thorn's house so he and his son can return home. Once they do, we can have some privacy here in my cabin."

"Don't you go getting your feathers ruffled, Chief," Red said. "Although I guess I did sound sort of demanding. Will it help if I say *please*?"

"I am not getting my 'feathers ruffled,' as you say. I meant exactly what I said. Ramona must stay here with you and Thorn as long as this girl-woman is here. Your people already say bad things about her because of her sister who is dead and the stolen child. She must be with another woman in the house as long as she stays here."

"You're absolutely right about that, old friend. I hadn't thought of people talking. I don't guess Jeannie has either. You go ahead then, Billy, and send Sheriff Logan up here pronto."

Billy and Emma rode out of the yard on matching bay mares, two of Will's brown horses.

Ramona led Jeannie up the ladder to the loft and tucked her into the blanket bed Billy had slept on since Red came home.

As soon as the girl seemed completely asleep, Ramona climbed down the ladder and headed for the stove, announcing in a soft voice, "I will make you some real food. You men eat too much fried bread and beans. You need meat and potatoes. Something to keep you strong and healthy."

"Thank you, my dear," Will said. "Red and I are going out to check on the horses while there's still a little daylight left. We'll be back shortly."

Standing beside his father with his elbows resting on the top rail of the corral, Red suddenly realized he stood a little taller than Will. Sometime while he wasn't paying attention, he'd shot up at least an inch over his father.

Red smiled when he thought of Ramona with his father and Emma with Chief Billy together in the cabin while he was gone. The whole situation tickled him. And all of them acted as if they'd dreaded his finding out.

"What are you smiling about, boy? I can't think of anything funny about this mess."

"I wasn't thinking about Patten and his crooks or even that poor little boy. There's little we can do about any of that at the moment. Not until we have some help. I was thinking about you and Billy trying to hide your love life from me."

"I'd as soon not talk about it, if you don't mind."

"Well, excuse me. I'll gladly leave it alone. I still say it's amusing."

Will made a snorting noise and turned away to walk back toward the cabin, muttering to himself.

Red leaned against the fence.

If I could remember the layout of the White Willow buildings and the floor plan of the house, it's possible I could slip in there. If I could, I might be able to get that kid and sneak back out without any kind of a fight.

I don't know. I might make things worse. I sure might make it worse if they caught me. Maybe I'd better wait for the sheriff. He'll surely be here in a few hours. That is, if he's in town. I sort of think he's up on the mountain, trying to figure out the tracks of those killers.

I just don't know. That poor little kid is probably terrified. Maybe I'd better go up there and at least have a look around. I might be able to spot where they're keeping the boy and figure out some way to get to him.

Someone lit a lamp in the cabin. As he walked back to go inside, Red could see Ramona and his father through the window. She stood close to the stove, stirring something, and Will set plates and glasses on the table.

Chapter Sixteen

When Red woke up the next morning, he knew what to do. Moving as quietly as he could, he put some split kindling into the firebox of the cookstove and sprinkled it with slivers of fat pine. On top of the kindling he piled in all the pieces of dry pine stove wood it would hold and dropped in a lighted match. When the blaze flared up, he slid the lid into place. Without waiting for the stove to heat, he filled the coffeepot with water, added a generous amount of coffee, and placed the pot on the hottest part of the stove.

He decided to shave while he waited for the coffee to boil. Filling a basin with warm water from the stove's reservoir, he stood at the worktable and bent his knees to bring his face even with the small mirror hung at a height comfortable for Chief Billy to shave.

When he finished shaving, he emptied the water into the slop bucket and refilled the basin to wash. As soon as he dried off, he dressed in a dark blue wool shirt and clean jeans, then sat down to pull on his boots.

When he heard the coffeepot rumbling, he rushed over to yank it to a cooler part of the stove before it boiled over. Grabbing a cup from the safe, he poured the coffee slowly to keep from getting any grounds into the cup, planning to enjoy it in the quiet.

Will spoke softly from the bottom bunk. "Pour me a cup of that coffee, son. It sure does smell good."

"Take this cup, Dad. I'll pour me another one."

"Thanks, son. What are you up to so early in the morning? It won't be full light for another hour."

"As soon as it gets light enough outside to see where I'm walking, I'm gonna hike over that ridge on the other side of the near pasture. I plan to see if I can sneak down through that mess of sycamore trees and elder bushes next to Falling Creek. I'll go along there where it runs close behind the White Willow ranch house.

"I think I might be able to get that boy out of there. I'm scared for a posse to ride in there shooting. If they do, that baby is just as liable to get killed as any of the outlaws.

"Not only that, Patten may figure on a posse coming and decide to take the kid somewhere away from the ranch to hide him. I can't let that happen, so I have to go soon."

"How come it has to be you doing this?"

"There's several reasons, I guess. One is, Joey is Wes and Becky's baby. I reckon I owe it to Becky, if not to Wes, to try to get the poor little fella back from Patten. Another reason, and I guess the biggest one, is that Jeannie came to me in her trouble. She asked me to help her.

"Actually, though, when I think it through, neither of those are the main reason I have to go try to find the boy. I have to go because I'm here and I can. Does that make sense to you, Dad?"

"You're a good man, son. I don't always agree with your thinking, but I'm proud of you."

"Thanks, Dad. It's good of you to say so. Look. I've got to get on my way. It's almost light. How about lending me that little peashooter of a gun you always carry in your boot? I've got my gun and my knife, but another hidden weapon can't hurt. You never know what you might run into."

"Of course you can use it. You'll be all right with it, since you'll be on foot. I had the devil's own time getting used to riding with the thing stuck down in my boot. Take the canteen hanging on the wall over top the wash bench as well. If you have to hide out for a spell, you may need it."

Red walked fast. When he crossed the pasture, Pitch tossed his head and ran toward him, but he ignored the horse and hurried toward the fence. At the top of the hill he dropped to the ground and rolled under the lowest strand of the barbed-wire fence. Pushing himself up with both hands, he stood and continued walking through the closely growing cedars.

Moving out into the open as the cedars thinned, he looked toward the White Willow ranch house, but the limbs of the thick sycamore trees were all he could see. As he trotted downhill, he soon left the scattered cedars and passed some clumps of rock. Several stood as tall as his shoulders. After the area of scattered rocks, he entered an open expanse. Cattle grazed contentedly, ignoring him as he walked by.

Patten didn't sell this herd of cows, at least—there must be two or three hundred head scattered out here. They probably like it near the water and shade.

Relieved to be back in the relative safety of the woods and brush surrounding the creek, Red slowed his pace to step carefully through the matted leaves. He wanted to avoid as much noise as possible when he approached the open area around the ranch compound, in case any of Patten's crew might be stirring.

When he reached the edge of the woods, he stopped to crouch in a thicket of box elders to search the corrals and barnyard for anyone moving around.

The sun was up. He could hear the sound of cattle moving into the trees behind him. They had eaten their fill of grass and wanted to lie down in the shade where it was cool.

More than an hour passed while he crouched there, and nobody moved within his sight. Sure no one was around, Red moved restlessly. He tensed, ready to leave his cover and run to the back door of the big barn, when two men came out of the bunkhouse and walked toward the stables.

After a few minutes the men came back out of the barn, each leading two saddled horses. When they disappeared around the end of the house, Red darted from the safety of the bushes and ran across the open space and through the back door of a smokehouse.

I'll hide in one of these outbuildings close to the house until it gets dark. I should be able to figure out where they're keeping little Joey. Once I know exactly where he is, I might be able to come up with some way to get him out of there.

The heat in the smokehouse stifled Red, and the smell of salt meat soon became overpowering. He felt an uncomfortable sensation in his empty stomach. He knelt on the dirt floor, peeping through a narrow crack left where the board door wasn't a tight fit.

I shoulda had enough sense to at least bring some jerky to chew on. Thank goodness Dad reminded me to bring this water. I'da forgot about it for sure if he hadn't said anything.

I may never want to eat ham or bacon again. This place stinks something awful. Maybe not never eat ham or bacon again—but not eat it for a long time. If it wasn't for this crack beside the door, I'd probably fall over in a faint, the air's so bad in here.

Wait a minute. That has to be Joey's crying I hear.

It's coming from the end room of the wing on the west side of the house. I can see somebody walking around inside the room—whoever it is passes by the window now and again. I can't see well enough to tell if it's a man or a woman.

I sure hope it's one of those women who work over there sometimes. They'd surely be gentle with the poor little guy. I don't figure Gilbert Patten or any of his men for having a whole lot of patience with a crying kid.

Red sat down on the dirt floor of the smokehouse to rest his legs, but he kept his nose and eyes pressed close to the crack beside the door.

After a while the baby quieted.

Red dozed off and on through the afternoon. When he woke, he watched for any activity inside or outside the house, but all stayed still and quiet. After several hours he heard Joey crying again, but the sound stopped quickly, as though someone was near him and caring for his needs.

As soon as it was dusk, Red slipped out of the smokehouse and hid behind some shrubbery growing close to the house. Crouching to make himself smaller and moving as silently as he could, he worked his way along the back of the main house to the corner where the addition joined it.

A light burned in the room where he heard the boy. No shrubbery grew along this part of the house for him to hide behind, so Red dropped to all fours below the level of the windows and crawled toward the light. He hoped to find the child alone so he could climb in through the window and rescue him.

Just as he reached the spot below the window and started to raise himself up to peep in, something struck him between his shoulder blades and knocked him against the wall of the house. An instant later his head felt as if it had exploded. Everything went blank as he crumpled to the ground.

Bright daylight shone in when Red woke up. He'd been knocked out or asleep all night.

He could smell dirt—plain dirt, not salt meat or dirt saturated with a century of salt used to cure meat. He lay on a packed dirt floor. Opening his eyes farther, he started to raise his head and winced with pain.

He could see part of a rough board stairway. It led up to a closed door. Turning his head, he saw that the light came in through two below-ground windows set in deep window wells. One of the windows stood open, propped up with a stick.

If I could get loose and get over there, I think I could climb out that window. No, I'll never get loose. These ropes are tied too tight.

And my boots are gone. Why in the Sam Hill would somebody take my boots?

It would take a sharp knife to get me loose—a knife to cut through the knots in these ropes. I'll never get them untied.

I must be in the basement of the main house. If I could at least sit up, I think I'd feel better.

Struggling, twisting, pushing against the dirt floor with his bound hands, Red finally worked himself into a sitting position.

Whew. What a job. I'm plumb worn out, and my head smarts like the dickens. Whoever hit me gave me a heck of a whack.

At least I don't feel sick or dizzy this time. I figure since I don't feel like puking, whoever hit me at least didn't give me another concussion.

I wonder why in the world somebody took my boots. So much for my knife and the little gun of Dad's.

It was still bright outside when the door at the top of the stairs rattled and was thrown open. Gilbert Patten and a squat, white-haired man Red didn't know stomped down the steps.

"How's your head feeling, Thornton?" Patten asked in a loud voice. "I hope Blackie here didn't hit you too hard. He says he tried to smash your head in with that rifle butt. I reckon you've just got a truly hard head."

The man Gilbert Patten called Blackie didn't say a word but stood close behind the outlaw leader and grinned, showing broken teeth.

Red didn't answer but stared at Patten. He'd seen the man several times in Acorn Creek. He looked older than he remembered. His dark hair and beard were shaggy, and both carried generous streaks of white. He wore a plaid wool shirt and new-looking pants tucked into the tops of Red's black boots.

"I see you admiring my new boots. They were a gift. The fella who used to wear 'em ain't gonna need 'em much longer, and I been needing me a new pair. I'm just lucky they're the right size.

"Me and Blackie are gonna ride outa here and go pay a visit to our old buddy Wes Lane at his big ranch way down in Guadalajara, in ol' Mexico. I'm sure he's lonesome for some friendly company by this time. He wrote me a letter saying he was coming home. I figure he'll be particular pleased to see us. I know he'll be plumb grateful to us for bringing him his little boy."

"What are you trying to prove, Patten? Why bring an innocent baby into your meanness?"

"Why, I ain't mean, Thornton, and, by thunder, I resent you saying such a thing to me. I should think you'd try to keep a civil tongue, considering your position. I ain't a bit mean. I just think different from people like you.

"I only came down here to ease your mind about that poor little kid upstairs. I knowed it was him you were after last night when Blackie caught you sneaking around behind the house. I bet you thought you was gonna rescue the little one and make yourself a big hero man with that fine-looking Jeannie McClain."

Patten and the man he called Blackie laughed aloud.

"Well, you won't be no great big hero when this place burns down on top of your head. That's exactly what I'm gonna do. I'm gonna take that kid to Wes and leave this here place a hole in the ground full of ashes. With a United States Marshal dead on the old trail, this place is no more use to me as a hideout.

"I might even decide to steal the kid back from Wes someday and bring him back to Miss Jeannie my own self. I been noticing her right along. She's about ripe, and I wouldn't mind breaking her in."

Red's eyes became mere slits. His hands itched to smash Patten's face. He knew he was helpless, and anything he said would be futile, so he refused to say anything.

Patten laughed aloud and said, "That's right, Thornton. You sit there and think on what'll happen when I leave this place. It might be tonight or maybe tomorrow night. You'll know I'm long gone when you hear those old pine logs start to snapping and popping right up there over your head.

"How long do you reckon the house will burn before the fire reaches you? Do you think you'll end up dying from breathing the smoke, or do you think you'll burn up?

"I hope you burn up like a piece of bacon left on the fire too long."

Still laughing, Patten and Blackie turned away from Red to climb the stairs and disappear through the door, shutting it firmly behind them.

Red closed his eyes.

I sure hope the smoke gets me and not the flames if that low-down scum actually sets fire to this house.

Straining and struggling, he worked his way over near a packing box so he'd have something to rest against. No more than five or ten minutes passed when he heard a noise at the open window.

Most of the fading light suddenly disappeared. Someone jumped down into the window well and began to crawl into the basement through the open window.

Red's heart pounded. He raised his head and watched, fascinated, as a man struggled to climb through the narrow open window. He finally stood up inside the basement and stretched to straighten his back.

That fellow's shape looks familiar—I wonder if it could be . . .

The man moved closer and removed his hat with one hand as he raised the other to his lips to motion for Red to keep silent.

It was Wes.

"You've got a nerve—you . . ."

"Keep it down, Red," he whispered. "I'll get these ropes off you."

"Where in the name of goodness did you come from, Wes?" Red whispered, his voice strained from excitement. "Why are you here?"

"Shush—keep it down, I said. Hold still. Those men may hear you.

"I got to Acorn Creek last night on the stage. I went over to the hotel to get a room, and Curly Benton told me about Gil Patten and his men taking little Joey away from Jeannie. I don't know what Patten's up to. He knew I was coming.

"I turned myself around, got back onto a horse, and hightailed it up here. I took a roundabout way nobody else knows, so Patten's men didn't see me ride in.

"I was hiding out there in the bushes, and I heard Patten and a couple of his men talking. It couldn't'a been more than five minutes ago. They talked about you some and said they would ride out to the main gate to make some sort of ransom demand to the sheriff and his posse.

"I heard Patten say that when they came back here, they're gonna take my son away and set fire to the house. We've got to find the boy and get out of here fast. They won't be away from the house long.

"Here, rub your legs some to start the circulation." Wes knelt to rub Red's left leg with both hands as Red rubbed the right.

"I'm okay, Wes. They didn't have the ropes wrapped tightly enough to make my legs go completely to sleep— they're just a little stiff and tingly.

"I know where your boy is, Wes, or at least where he was early last night. They kept him in the last room in the west wing, the one closest to the back door. Can we go through the house to get around to that room?"

"You're darn right we can. If we're lucky, nobody will be up there but Ruth Gordon and her daughter, Jill. I know they're here—I saw their buggy sitting out by the barn. They won't try to stop us. Neither one of those women is worth the powder and shot it would take to blow 'em to kingdom come, but they wouldn't hurt a little kid."

Wes was at the top of the stairs. Red ran right behind him, limping on legs set on fire by returning circulation.

Wes pushed the door open and looked both ways. "Come on. The coast is clear."

Wes ran on tiptoe to avoid making too much noise when his boot heels hit the floor. Red felt strange running in his stocking feet. He stepped carefully to keep from slipping on the polished wood floors.

When they reached the door of the room where Red remembered hearing Joey crying, Wes never hesitated. He reached one hand out to turn the knob and threw the door open as he stepped through.

An elderly black woman sat in a rocking chair, holding the baby in her arms, swaying back and forth and humming. A younger woman Red assumed was Ruth Gordon's daughter, Jill, jumped up from the bed and let out a shriek.

"Mr. Wes! Where'd you come from? You about scared me to death, busting in here like that!"

"Keep your voice down, Jill, for heaven's sake. You too, Ruth. Give me the boy. We're leaving right now. You two stay put in this room and keep quiet, or I'll come back here one night, and you'll both be sorry."

Joey woke and started screaming at the top of his lungs.

Patting the boy's back to calm him, Wes pushed open the window and stepped through. As soon as his feet touched the ground, he started to run as fast as he could while holding the child, leading the way toward the woods near the creek.

Just before they entered the comparative safety of the woods, Red looked back to see three men standing near the house. The older black woman joined them and raised a hand to point their way.

"Run, Wes. They see us, and they're coming."

All three men held rifles. They raised them to their shoulders and started to shoot as Wes and Red entered the woods.

Red heard bullets sing past him. Seconds later one found Wes. He lurched forward to his knees, blood pouring down his arm.

"Take the boy, Red. Here—take him, quick. I can make it if you carry him. My rifle is right up there in the first bunch of rocks. Take my son, and get him to where he's safe."

Red picked up the howling baby, clasped him against his chest with one arm, and turned to run as hard as he could through the woods. As he approached the rocks, he looked back.

Wes was running again, bent low, with one hand pressed against his wounded shoulder. When he reached the rocks, he grabbed his rifle and knelt behind the rock and dirt shelf.

Turning, he almost screamed, "Go on! Please, go on, Red—run! Get the boy to safety. I'll be all right. I can hold them off. Sheriff Logan will hear the shooting and bring the posse. Go, please. Don't let Patten get his hands on my son again."

Red's stocking feet slipped on the rocks as he hurried up the slope, sometimes using his free hand to help himself along. When he reached the shelter of the cedars, he heard the shooting start again. It sounded like four or five rifles firing at once. Pushing himself as hard as he could on his torn feet, he raced through the cedars.

When he left the cedars and started downhill, he put Joey down on the ground to roll under the barbed wire. Standing again, he reached over and picked up the sobbing boy. Terrified, Joey wrapped both arms around Red's neck in an infant choke hold.

Red started yelling when he reached the middle of the pasture.

Chapter Seventeen

Ramona and Jeannie met him at the corral fence. Jeannie held her arms out for Joey. As soon as the baby saw Jeannie, he loosed his hold on Red's neck and fell against her. She clasped him to her chest and sat down on the ground, sobbing her relief.

"Red—Red—oh, thank you—thank you!"

"I'll talk later, Jeannie. I have to go back."

Turning away, he ran toward the house.

Ramona ran behind him, screaming, "Stop, Red—stop! Your feet are bleeding. You're leaving blood with every step you take, Sit down, and let me tend to your feet. You'll kill yourself."

"Not now, Ramona. Not now. I have to go back. I'll wear Dad's old boots."

Sticking one long arm under the bottom bunk, Red

pulled out a pair of worn brown leather boots, then turned to sit on the bunk and pull them onto his feet. He winced at the pain in his lacerated skin as he walked across the cabin to take Billy's extra rifle from the corner nearest the door.

He knew the rifle would be loaded, but he rummaged in the drawer of the kitchen safe to find two unopened boxes of shells. Tearing the boxes open, he filled the pockets of his jeans.

Ignoring Ramona's frantic pleas to stop and let her bandage his feet, Red hurried out the door and back up the hill. When he reached the cedars again, he couldn't hear the rifles.

That can only mean only one of two things: Wes is down, or he's out of ammunition. At least five or six men were at the ranch with Patten. They would never just quit.

When he reached the open area beyond the cedars, Red saw Sheriff Logan kneeling beside someone lying on the ground near the clump of rocks and dirt Wes had sheltered behind. Andrew McClain and Leon Jackson stood nearby, holding rifles.

Beyond the group of men he could see two bodies lying in the open field. Two mounted men seemed to be just waiting for something to happen.

"How bad is he, Sheriff?" Red asked as he reached the rocks.

Logan shook his head. "He's gone, Thornton. Those low-down skunks shot him at least ten times."

Red dropped to his knees beside Logan to stare at Wes' still face. Sadness filled his chest with a burning pressure. "He came through in the end, Logan. He saved my life and rescued his boy from those devils. I just left Joey with Jeannie over at Billy's cabin."

"That ain't all he done. He told us the truth about what happened in the alley when Johnny Yates got killed. McClain and Leon here heard every word he said.

"He told us the story exactly like you told it, Thornton. He said you were knocked plumb out and didn't know a thing when he pulled your handgun and killed Yates. That he shot Johnny because Yates came outside and saw him holding up a big rock, ready to bash your brains out."

"Well, praise be for it."

"I reckon you would say 'praise be.' I know I'd be saying that and more besides. I'll be able to get you a full pardon from the governor, Red. I'll write everything out and get McClain and Leon to witness it. The pardon will be near about automatic."

"I guess Wes just took longer than most fellas do to grow up."

"I'd say you're a whole lot more generous than I could ever be, but the man is dead. I don't reckon your going around resenting what he did to you would have any profit in it now."

"Will you get somebody to have Martindale come up here and get him, Sheriff? He should be buried down in town. I expect there's a place for him beside the major in the church cemetery."

"His little boy will be able to know his daddy was a hero, I reckon," Sheriff Logan said as he stood up. "There's no need of telling the kid anything else."

Red slipped off his jacket and covered Wes's face.

As soon as he stood up, he turned to ask Sheriff Logan, "Do you think you could find me a horse to ride back over to Billy's place?"

"I sure can. What happened to you, anyway? I noticed you walking kinda funny. Did you take a bullet when Patten and his cronies chased you and Wes?"

"I wasn't shot. I'm fine. Patten and his men took my boots when they tied me up and threw me into the basement of the ranch house. My left boot must be full of blood, the way it's squishing every time I take a step. I ran to Billy's cabin, in my stocking feet."

"My goodness. No wonder you asked for a horse."

Logan turned to his deputy. "Leon, go catch up one of those loose horses for Red." He turned back to Red. "While we're waiting for Leon to catch that horse, Thornton, I'd like to tell you what your father and Billy Two Horses did a little while ago."

"What do you mean, what Dad and Chief Billy did?"

"Don't worry, they're both fine. They just decided my posse might get you killed, and they made it to the main gate of the ranch before we did.

"When McClain here and about twenty other men rode up to the White Willow gate, mad as a swarm of hornets and loaded for bear, there sat your dad and Billy, still mounted, each with a rifle trained on the posse.

"They'd gotten the drop on Patten's guards somehow or another. The two men sat on the ground with their backs to fence posts, tied up like hogs ready for slaughter. The posse rode up to the gate, all hot under the collar. I reckon McClain here mighta been the worst, but most of the men got pretty well fired up. It ain't often anybody bothers with a little kid, and the men were in a state about it."

Logan paused before continuing. "Your dad and Billy ordered them to halt and threatened to start shooting if they tried to get past them. McClain and a couple of the men told me they felt no doubt they would have been shot out of their saddles if they had dared to try anything."

Logan shook his head. "I was about ten minutes behind the posse. I waited to send another telegram to the marshal's office, telling them what was going on and asking them to get up here and help me.

"When I got to the gate, Billy didn't say anything, but your dad told me flat-out, the posse wasn't gonna go in shooting until you got out of there.

"I tried making noises about me representing the law and talking about what kind of trouble he and Billy would be in if they didn't let me through that gate, when we heard the shooting start down here. It was far away at first and stopped pretty quick for a minute or two, but it started up again right smart.

"Your dad and Billy didn't say a word but opened the gate, turned their horses, and led us right through."

"Where are Dad and Billy now?"

"They're out with the rest of the posse trying to find that doggone Gil Patten. I'm fairly certain we got all of his men either shot or rounded up, but Patten slipped out of sight some kind of way, and they're beating the bushes for him.

"I thought at first he'd gone for the boat, but it's still there, tied up at the dock like always. We finally decided he got his hands on a horse and took off.

"I told the men to scatter and find him. Patten needs to be caught. If he should get away clean, he'll just start up his meanness somewhere else."

"Or he'll get another gang together and come back here and cause trouble for everybody just for spite," Red said.

"I hadn't thought of that, but I guess it's sure enough something that could happen."

Logan looked up. "Here's Leon with an extra horse for you, Red. I think I'll ride along with you. I'm sure McClain wants to go with us. He'll want to see Jeannie and the boy."

Red called to Andrew McClain, "Come on and ride with us, Mr. McClain. I'm heading for Chief Billy's place. That's where Jeannie and Joey are."

"I'm obliged, Thornton."

Andrew McClain moved closer and held out his right hand. "I'm obliged to you for getting the boy out of there, Red. I know he's safe, but I'll believe it for sure when I get to see him."

"I know what you mean. I'd sort of like to see my dad and that ding-busted Billy Two Horses about now my own self."

McClain climbed into the saddle, and the four men walked their horses through the open area where several bodies lay.

Sheriff Logan called to two members of the posse and told them to stay there and keep watch. "I'll send the undertaker up here. He'll probably make it early tomorrow morning. As soon as he gets here, you can come on in."

The men looked glum at the prospect of spending a night in the open with no company but several dead men, but they nodded in agreement.

Pulling the heavy main gate closed after the group passed through, Red noticed two ropes lying on the ground beside two fence posts.

"Did those two get away?"

"Nah—a couple of men from the posse took them on down to town. They'll be locked up in my jail when I get back to my office."

"How many men do you think Patten had?"

"Gosh darn if I know for sure. I think we shot six. Those two guards make eight, besides Patten himself. I can't tell you if that's all we shot or how many might have gotten away."

"That's sort of a scary thought."

"You bet it is. I'll feel a lot better if someone from that posse comes in with Patten facedown across his saddle."

"I think I agree with you."

Sheriff Logan rode beside Red without speaking for almost a mile. When they reached the corner of Billy's pasture fence, he asked, "Is this the start of Billy Two Horses' land?"

"It sure is."

"That's a nice, strong fence he's got."

"He's kept my and dad's horses in here since I went to Yuma. I expect he and Dad did a lot of work to keep it in good shape."

"I hear a horse whistling."

"I do too. It sounds like my Pitch. There's a gate down the hill there. I'd better go see what's bothering him."

"We'll all go. He sounds sort of excited to me. It might be a painter after your young stock. It could even be somebody down there bothering him."

Too concerned to speak further, Red nudged his borrowed horse with both knees to urge him to a fast trot.

When they stopped before the gate, Leon jumped off his mount, yanked the wire closure off the top of the end pole, and pulled the gate open enough to lead the horses through. When they were all inside the pasture, he pushed the gate closed and slipped the wire back into place.

All four men urged their horses to a gallop. When

they crested a small hill, they could see an excited Pitch swinging his head and leaping about in an apparent frenzy of anger. He stood on his hind legs and whistled his displeasure every time his feet came down. A long rope hung from his neck.

Red stopped his mount well back and stepped to the ground, still holding Billy's rifle. His feet hurt so much, he almost fell when he tried to take the first step. Gritting his teeth, he limped toward the stallion, talking softly to calm the horse.

Pitch began to quiet as soon as he saw Red. He bounced up and down on stiff front legs several times but stopped whistling his anger.

Placing one hand on the horse's sweaty side, Red loosened the noose from his neck and slipped it over his head. As soon as he knew he was free of the rope, the stallion danced around several times, threw up his heels, and galloped for the barn.

"I always heard folks say nobody could ride him but you, Red. I guess Patten didn't believe it."

"Hey, Red, look over there against that little oak. Isn't that Gil Patten?"

"By all that's holy, it is. Is he dead?"

Leon stepped in between Red and Sheriff Logan and announced in a loud voice, "Thornton, if that wild horse of yours killed Patten, he'll have to be shot. It don't matter none that Patten's an outlaw. Any horse that kills a man has got to be put down."

"Leon, you just back the heck off. I don't care if the man is dead ten times over. Nobody's putting Pitch down."

"Don't fight, boys," Logan said, stretching out one arm to point. "Look, Patten's not dead—he's up."

"Hurry, catch him before he gets into that brush."

Patten stopped and dropped behind a small clump of brush, firing one shot at the group of men.

Sheriff Logan fell heavily, yelling as he hit the ground, "Don't stop—get him!"

Leon and McClain dropped to the ground beside the sheriff.

Forgetting his wounded feet, Red took two long jumps to crouch behind the small oak. Raising the rifle to his shoulder, he swept the clump of bushes with fire. Patten screamed and fell, his gun falling from his hand.

"Is the sheriff all right?" Red called out.

"I'm fine, Red. He didn't shoot me. I just tripped. I'll be all right soon's I find my hat. It looks like you did for the fool."

"You're right—Patten's a fool. He's not hurt bad either. I guess I just grazed his head—looks like he's coming around."

"Get over there and put handcuffs on him, Leon," Logan ordered. "Not with his hands in front—don't you know nothing? Turn him over, and pull his hands around behind him. A prisoner can do too much if you put the handcuffs on him in front. He might even figure out some trick to get away."

Patten's eyes opened. He shook his head to clear it and stared up at Red with such malevolence, Red felt compelled to turn his eyes away.

"I'll get that devil of a black horse someday, Thornton," Patten growled.

Leon dragged Patten roughly to his feet and pushed him toward Logan.

The sheriff grabbed the outlaw's arm and said, "Just shut your mouth, Patten. You're not gonna get anything but a rope. We found enough evidence on your men to prove your gang is guilty of robbing stages and banks and killing people all around the area. A United States Marshal will be in Acorn Creek to take you into custody in less than a week. You're not gonna be getting anybody for anything."

Logan turned to his deputy. "Leon, get him up onto your horse. We'll transfer him to this one Thornton's riding as soon as we get to Chief Billy's cabin. Red's in no shape to walk the rest of the way, and you are. Lead the horse along behind us."

Jeannie and Ramona hurried out of the house when they rode into the yard. When Red slid out of the saddle to stand on the ground, Jeannie ran straight into his arms.

"Joey's asleep. He's all right." She started to sob again, "You wouldn't let me thank you—I was so scared."

"Stop crying, Jeannie. It's all right. Everything's all right. We even captured Patten—with Pitch's help."

"Sit right down where you are, and take those boots

off, Rufus Thornton. You can romance that girl later." Ramona's voice was stern. She stood at Red's elbow, holding a basin of steaming water and some bandages.

"Yes, ma'am," Red answered, grinning down at Jeannie.